"You have **he went o**ⁿ~~~~~~~~~~~ **down divine judgment. "You can serve your sentence in a jail cell or you can serve it as my queen."**

Guinevere clasped her hands together to stop them from shaking. Her throat closed. Yes, the Accorsis were terrible, she knew that. That was why she'd stayed hidden all these years, as much as she was able, and that was why she'd been desperate to escape. Except she hadn't escaped. She let herself be trapped by her family's enemy, and now she was facing a jail cell for crimes she hadn't committed.

Silence lay heavy over the throne room, smoke from the recently put-out fire in one corner filling the space with an ashy smell.

Tiberius hadn't looked away from her, not once.

She felt almost crushed by the pressure of his gaze.

Jackie Ashenden writes dark, emotional stories with alpha heroes who've just gotten the world to their liking only to have it blown apart by their kick-ass heroines. She lives in Auckland, New Zealand, with her husband, the inimitable Dr. Jax, two kids and two rats. When she's not torturing alpha males and their gutsy heroines, she can be found drinking chocolate martinis, reading anything she can lay her hands on, wasting time on social media or being forced to go mountain biking with her husband. To keep up-to-date with Jackie's new releases and other news, sign up to her newsletter at jackieashenden.com.

Books by Jackie Ashenden

Harlequin Presents

His Innocent Unwrapped in Iceland
A Vow to Redeem the Greek
Spanish Marriage Solution
Newlywed Enemies

Three Ruthless Kings

Wed for Their Royal Heir
Her Vow to Be His Desert Queen
Pregnant with Her Royal Boss's Baby

The Teras Wedding Challenge

Enemies at the Greek Altar

Scandalous Heirs

Italian Baby Shock
The Twins That Bind

Work Wives to Billionaires' Wives

Boss's Heir Demand

Visit the Author Profile page
at Harlequin.com for more titles.

KING, ENEMY, HUSBAND

JACKIE ASHENDEN

H Harlequin

PRESENTS

Harlequin® PRESENTS™

ISBN-13: 978-1-335-93988-3

King, Enemy, Husband

Copyright © 2025 by Jackie Ashenden

For questions and comments about the quality of this book, please contact us at CustomerService@Harlequin.com.

TM and ® are trademarks of Harlequin Enterprises ULC.

 Harlequin Enterprises ULC
22 Adelaide St. West, 41st Floor
Toronto, Ontario M5H 4E3, Canada
www.Harlequin.com

Printed in Lithuania

Recycling programs for this product may not exist in your area.

MIX
Paper | Supporting responsible forestry
FSC® C021394

KING, ENEMY, HUSBAND

To Soraya. I miss the GIFs already. :)

CHAPTER ONE

TIBERIUS MAXIMUS BENEDICTUS of the House of Aquila, in approximately five minutes from now the newly crowned and rightful King of Kasimir, strode down the wide hallway to the throne room, a flock of men consisting of his aides, guards, one general and a priest following on his wake.

The coup that had finally ousted the Accorsi tyrants hadn't been as bloodless as he'd wanted—there had been casualties, though thankfully no civilians had been hurt—but at least his strategies had paid off.

Finally, after twenty years of Accorsi rule that had nearly brought the country to the brink of collapse, the Accorsis had been defeated. And now they were gone. For good.

The one black spot in his otherwise unblemished victory was that unfortunately the Accorsis had managed to evade capture, and the last report he'd received was that they'd fled Kasimir entirely. Much to his fury.

He'd hoped to bring Renzo Accorsi and his advisors before the courts here, to answer for their crimes, but sadly that was not an option. Still, the international authorities had been notified. Renzo would be brought to justice in time, Tiberius had no doubt.

First, though, and most important, was the crown.

He wouldn't be King until it was on his head, and only once it was could he start with the vital work of rebuilding the country that years of mismanagement and civil unrest had torn apart. Nothing was more important than that. Nothing.

The empty hallway echoed with the sound footsteps on the ancient parquet of the floor as Tiberius and his entourage swept into the throne room.

Or at least what remained of the throne room.

It had been home to the rulers of Kasimir in various iterations for centuries. The Accorsi coup that had ousted his parents and caused the death of his mother had occurred when he'd been a baby, so he had never been inside it himself...

Until now.

Growing up in Italy, hidden and forgotten, his father would often bring Tiberius to the mountains that looked over Kasimir. There had been a scenic lookout spot where tourists could pull off the road and take pictures of the picture-perfect European castle and jagged, snow-capped mountains that surrounded it.

'*That* is your legacy, boy,' his father would tell him, pointing at the castle spires. '*That* is yours. *That* is where you belong.'

Well. Now he was here.

In the castle that had been taken from him and his family years before.

His true home.

Tiberius paused in the doorway, then scowled.

The throne room was a bloody mess.

In their rush to leave, the Accorsis had somehow found the time to get their soldiers to desecrate the Kasimiran throne room.

Most of the tapestries had been torn down and were lying in heaps near the walls. Centuries-old paintings were scored and cut with knives. The panelled oak that lined the walls had been kicked in and spray-painted with obscenities, and someone had even tried to light a fire in one corner with the remains of an ornate chair. Smoke drifted across the pitted parquet as one of Tiberius's own guards hurried to douse the fire with water.

Tiberius scanned the mess, trying to rein in his fury at the mess. Because a good strategist never let his feelings get in the way and certainly neither did a king. He turned to one of his aides, issued some sharp orders to get the clean-up started, then strode towards the dais and the huge carved oak throne that sat on top of it.

It was ancient, that throne, the wood smooth and dark with age and wear. The cushions that had likely been on the seat lay slashed open and scattered around the dais, feathers dusting the wood.

Tiberius ignored them as he climbed the stairs of the dais and kicked the remains of the cushions aside. A throne wasn't meant to be padded or comfortable, because once a king was comfortable that was where corruption lay. He wouldn't fall into that trap.

Slowly he turned and sat on the throne.

Finally.

After so long, a Benedictus sat on the throne once more. Now the ghosts of his parents could rest.

A deep, savage satisfaction curled through him, and he let himself feel it for a few seconds, because the road had been hard and long to get here. Years of training in other countries' armies to hone his military skills. Years of planning and political manoeuvring to gather supporters to his cause. Years of anguish watching his people suffer under Accorsi rule...

Now that was done.

Now the real work would begin.

Shoving aside the satisfaction, Tiberius snapped his fingers at the priest and another aide standing in the crowd clustered at the base of the dais.

'Father Domingo,' he said curtly. 'If you please?'

The aide holding the heavy gold circlet carved with oak leaves that was the Kasimir royal crown handed it to the priest, who immediately came up the stairs.

There would be no ceremony, no pomp and definitely no circumstance in this coronation. Tiberius didn't have time for any. His country needed hospitals and schools and new housing, not pointless and expensive ceremonies.

The priest intoned the words of an old prayer, then placed the circlet on Tiberius's brow. And just like that, after twenty years of exile, the crown of Kasimir finally rested on the head of the true King.

Tiberius ignored the weight of it, and this time allowed himself no satisfaction at all. Instead, he waited stoically as the little gathering of people at the foot of the dais cheered and applauded before raising his hand. Silence fell instantly.

He was not a man to be disobeyed.

'In my first act as King,' he began. 'I will—' He broke off abruptly, the back of his neck prickling.

Ten long years of military training had given him sharp senses and a finely honed awareness of threats. He was very aware of when he was being watched, for example, and he was definitely being watched now. And not only by the people gathered in the throne room.

Below him, one of his guards shifted on his feet, boots scuffing on the parquet.

'Quiet!' Tiberius snapped, trying to concentrate on the prickling sensation, scanning the room while his men waited in absolute silence.

Everything was the way it had been before he'd come in here. Nothing had changed. He glanced up at the ceiling to find nothing but painted plaster. Nowhere for anyone to watch him from there, clearly.

Yet, the fact remained that he was being watched.

Like his father, he had a photographic memory, and as part of his training to take back the throne his father had made him memorise the palace floor plans. He knew that one of the Kings in centuries past had constructed a small network of narrow corridors within the thick palace walls, so his spies could secretly observe people.

Perhaps whoever it was, was in there?

Tiberius scanned the wall to his left. One of those corridors lay behind it, if he wasn't much mistaken, and there was a door to it behind one of heavy tapestries.

Well, whoever was lurking in those corridors wouldn't stay hidden for long. Not if he had anything to do with it.

Saying anything would alert whoever was hiding, so he didn't speak, merely glanced at his captain of the guard and jerked his head in the direction of the tapestry. The man knew all his king's wordless commands and instantly strode over to it and jerked aside the heavy fabric. A small, narrow door lay behind it, just as Tiberius suspected. The captain pulled open the door and disappeared into the corridor behind. A soft cry came through the doorway, then a scuffle of footsteps, and an instant later, much to Tiberius's surprise, the captain marched a slip of a girl all in white lace and muslin out into the throne room and over to the dais.

No, not a girl. A woman. A small woman, wearing some kind of flouncy, lacy white dress with a ragged hem and covered in dust. Her hair was a pale mass of curls, half falling out of a pink ribbon and hanging down her back, almost obscuring her face, but from what he could glimpse her features were delicate, precise and sharp.

She was very pale. Was it fear? If so then she *should* be afraid. She might not look like an immediate threat, but she'd been hiding in the walls and watching him, and that he would not tolerate.

His captain, who was holding her by her upper arm, released her, and she made an aggrieved sound, rubbing at her arm as she stood at the foot of dais.

The oddest thought crossed Tiberius's mind then... That she looked like a piece of thistledown coming down to rest on the old parquet of the floor. Either that or a terrified fairy—and, despite that aggrieved noise, she was definitely terrified.

Tiberius stared down at her impassively from his throne.

Who was she and why had she been in those secret corridors? Was she an Accorsi assassin, left behind to launch a surprise attack? Or an Accorsi spy, lying in wait to take back information on the new King?

Whatever she was, she wouldn't be doing it for much longer. She would go before the courts to be tried. The Accorsis and their hangers-on would answer for their crimes. He would make them.

'So,' he said at length. 'I see we have mice in the walls.'

The woman stared up at him, her sharp cheekbones pale as snow. Her curls had fallen back from her face, revealing a pair of the deepest, most luminous blue eyes he'd ever seen.

Something unfamiliar twisted in his gut and he found himself leaning forward, as if to study her more closely. There was fear in them, and yet an odd kind of defiance too.

Intriguing.

She'd been caught spying on him in his newly acquired throne room so she was right to be afraid. Yet this defiance in spite of her fear... It either made her very brave or very stupid.

'A silent mouse,' he murmured. 'You should speak, little mouse. Explain what you're doing, hiding and spying on your king.'

The fine line of her jaw hardened even though fear

still lurked in her eyes. 'I am not a mouse,' she said. 'And I was not spying.'

Her voice was precise and clear as glass.

'Then what were you doing?' He studied her intently, looking for signs of a lie, looking for weaknesses. He had a soldier's instinct, alert to anything and everything that might be a threat, and while she might not be an obvious one, looks could be deceiving.

A woman in a flouncy, lacy dress could still cause him problems, no matter how pretty she was—and he had to admit she was very pretty.

Not that he was interested. He had been sexually abstinent for the past six months as he'd entered the final stages of his plan to reclaim the throne, because he'd wanted no distractions. His body hadn't been happy about it, but he was a master of physical control and it would do what he wished.

Perhaps after his project for rebuilding Kasimir had got underway he'd find himself a willing woman and lose himself for a night or two. But not until then.

Everything had to wait until then.

The woman was holding herself very still, her hands clasped tightly together, and it was clear that she did not like being looked at the way he was looking at her.

Good. She wasn't supposed to like it. If she hadn't wanted to be looked at, she shouldn't have been hiding in the walls.

'Well?' He kept his tone calm, almost gentle. 'You will give me an answer, mouse. And that is an order, not a request.'

Her mouth firmed. 'I was…hiding.'

'Obviously. And who were you hiding from? My soldiers? Or...' Tiberius stopped as a thought came to him. Now he'd taken a good look at her, he saw there was an odd familiarity to her features, as if he'd seen a face like hers before, somewhere...

Yes. He knew where. The photos his father had kept, which he'd showed to Tiberius as he was growing up. Making sure Tiberius memorised the people in them. Making sure he knew who they were and what they'd done.

'These are your enemies,' his father had said. 'Your mother died because of them. Remember them. They took what is ours and it is up to you to get it back.'

Those sharp features, those blue eyes, that pale hair...

She was an Accorsi—of course she was.

A pulse of something hot and fierce lanced through him. So. Not all of them had escaped. One had stayed and here she was, standing before his reclaimed throne.

His prisoner.

His war prize.

'Miss Accorsi,' he said softly, watching her, seeing the flicker of shock in her eyes as he said the name, the delicate rosebud of her mouth opening. 'It is a dangerous thing for someone with your name to be hiding in walls.'

She went even paler, almost the colour of her dusty white dress. 'How do you know—?'

'You're Guinevere Accorsi, are you not?' he interrupted, because she had to be. Renzo had had three children and there was only one girl.

Her gaze flickered, then that sharp little chin of hers lifted, as if she was trying to stare him down, no matter that he was on a throne, on a dais, and she was at his feet.

'Y-Yes,' she said. 'And?'

Tiberius's grip on the arms of his throne tightened as a thought began to take shape in his head. He was a master strategist, all his risks calculated, his gambles fully with the odds in his favour. Being an excellent tactician had given him the crown that was by rights truly his and, while he didn't like surprises, when one presented itself he had no problem adapting it to suit his purposes.

If this woman was indeed Renzo's daughter, then she could be useful to him. There were still those sympathetic to the Accorsis scattered throughout the country—supporters who would no doubt cause trouble now he was King.

He could crush those pockets of resistance, jail the supporters or exile them from the country, but... The Accorsis had done exactly that when they'd taken power, and he was determined not to be like them. He refused. His country didn't need a tyrant intent on suppressing any protest. It needed to heal, and so did his people. The divides needed to be bridged, not deepened.

Which was where the Accorsi daughter came in.

Eventually he would need a queen, and while obtaining one had been the very last thing on his mind certainly when his first priority had been claiming his throne, she was here now and his prisoner. A Benedictus/Accorsi marriage would be the kind of union that Kasimir needed. It would unite the divided families and factions and would categorically underline his intentions for the country going forward.

No more divisions. Only peace and healing for his people.

Guinevere Accorsi was eyeing him warily, as if he was an unknown and potentially dangerous animal—and, to be fair, she was right to view him that way.

He *was* dangerous.

He stared back, turning over the idea slowly in his head. Yes, she was very pretty, but she would definitely need some styling if she was to be Kasimir's queen.

You will also need her consent to the marriage.

Of course. But he would get that. If he gave her a choice between being Queen and a prison cell, he was sure she'd choose the former rather than the latter.

Her eyes were startlingly blue against her white skin, and deep within them he could see her fear looking back at him.

Too bad. She was an Accorsi, of the same wretched lineage responsible for his mother's death and his country's near collapse. The things Renzo had done as King had been appalling, and while this little mouse might not have had a hand in any of it, she was still representative of the corruption that had lived in the heart of Kasimir for far too long.

He had no sympathy for her whatsoever.

Still, there was no reason to be unduly threatening. Not when it would serve no purpose. And he wasn't a man who did anything without purpose.

'In that case,' he said, after a long period of silence. 'I have a job for you.'

Her eyes widened. 'What kind of job?'

Tiberius held her gaze. 'Being my queen.'

Guinevere had watched Tiberius first enter the throne room from within the walls, safe in her little hiding place.

The enemy was here.

In the days leading up to his entry into Kasimir she'd overheard her father talking about him, calling him trivial, a minor annoyance that he would soon be rid of. Ineffectual and weak, like all the Benedictus family. One look at the Accorsi army and he'd be yelping his way back to Italy with his tail between his legs, Renzo had added.

It hadn't happened that way. Obviously. In fact, her father and her two older brothers had been in such a rush to flee the palace no one had bothered to check on her, and so she'd been able to slip away unnoticed into the secret corridors. She'd waited there, hiding, as her father, her brothers and the remaining guards who were still loyal had all escaped. Leaving her behind.

The relief she'd felt in that moment had been so intense she hadn't been able to quite believe it was real— that she'd finally managed to do what she'd dreamed of doing for so many years: being free of her family.

All she'd needed to do was to slip out through the corridors—no one in her family knew of their existence— and then the palace, and then she'd lose herself in the city streets and just…disappear.

Then he'd walked in and ruined it all.

Tiberius Maximus Benedictus, the rightful King of Kasimir.

She'd watched him sit on the throne, and then watched as the golden crown was lowered onto his short, inky black hair. He wore that crown as if he was wearing cloth of gold and robes of state, not grey army fatigues.

He wasn't exactly handsome—his face was all blunt planes and angles, and deeply carved into hard granite lines—but there was an aura about him that set him apart from other men. An aura of power, of a command so overwhelming that she'd almost felt it seeping through the walls to where she hid.

Utterly terrifying.

She should have made her escape then, while the coronation was happening, but she hadn't. She'd been caught, held fast despite her fear, by some kind of fascination she couldn't adequately describe. Perhaps it had something to do with finally seeing him, this famous enemy of her family, in the flesh and finding him to be not at all what she'd imagined.

This wasn't the beaten dog her father had kept saying he would shoot.

This was a man in total command of himself and his men and he was frightening.

Then his head had turned and he'd stared straight at her, as if he could see through the walls to where she hid, and she'd frozen. His eyes were a light silvery grey, pale and cold as winter snow, standing out starkly beneath his straight black brows and against his olive skin, and they were scalpel-sharp. Being stared at so intently had made her feel as if he was cutting away pieces of her soul, leaving the small, vulnerable parts at the centre of her exposed.

It had scared her so completely that she'd been left trembling. She'd told herself that of course he couldn't see her, and anyway it was time to leave and make her escape. But then, as she'd crept along the hidden corridor towards the exit, the door behind the tapestry had opened and one of his guards had seized her, dragging her before his throne.

She'd almost been sick with fear, while he'd sat there, legs spread arrogantly and that unnerving gaze of his pinning her to the spot. Yet beneath her terror had been a thread of unfamiliar anger too—at him, for finding her before she could disappear, and at herself, for lingering when she shouldn't have.

Hiding was what she did best—she'd been doing it for the past fifteen years—and yet when staying hidden had mattered the most, she'd failed.

Now she was here, standing before the new King, who was now demanding that she be his queen.

She could hardly process it, what with all the fear coursing through her body.

'Wh-What?' she stammered. 'Marry me? Why?'

He didn't move, didn't even blink. 'You are an Accorsi.'

'Yes, but—'

'There are divisions in this country,' he interrupted curtly. 'Deep divides that have hurt Kasimir. And as of today, those divisions will be no more. Your father was responsible for creating them, and since he is not here it will be you who will fix them.'

His voice was deep, resonant and utterly implacable, and something in it made her shiver.

'But I...' She stopped, then tried again. 'I—I can't be your queen.'

'You will.' He said the words as if it was a foregone conclusion. 'The Accorsis nearly destroyed this country, and since Renzo fled rather than face justice, you will answer for his crimes.'

Shock began to move through her in an icy wave. It was true that Renzo was a monster, as were her two older brothers—she'd been the butt of their worst behaviour over the years and they were the reasons she'd never ventured beyond the palace grounds.

It wasn't because she loved living here.

No, she hated it. And all she'd ever wanted to do was leave.

'But I didn't do anything,' she protested, barely able to get out the words she was so afraid. 'I never—'

'You are part of the Accorsi family.' He was relentless, cold as ice. 'Therefore you are complicit. Which means you *will* serve the sentence on behalf of your family.'

A ray of sun shone through the windows on either side of the throne, catching on the golden tips of the crown and glossing his coal-black hair. He looked utterly removed from anything as base as humanity. Untouchable, remote...god-like, almost.

'You have a choice, Guinevere Accorsi,' he went on, a warrior angel handing down divine judgment. 'You can serve your sentence in a jail cell or you can serve it as my queen.'

Guinevere clasped her hands together more tightly to stop them from shaking.

Complicit, he'd said. Cowardly, he'd said.

Her throat closed. Cowardly, yes—she already knew that. But complicit in what? She had no idea. She'd been held a prisoner in the palace since she was a child and knew nothing of the outside world. Her only escape was the books she read.

She'd been hoping that today would be her escape physically, too—except it hadn't. She'd let herself be trapped by her family's enemy, and now she was facing a jail cell for crimes she hadn't committed.

Crimes she knew nothing about.

Because you spent the last fifteen years hiding.

Guinevere shivered. She'd hidden, yes, but there were reasons for that. Very good reasons.

Silence lay heavy over the throne room, the smoke from the recently put-out fire in one corner filling the space with an ashy smell.

Tiberius hadn't looked away from her—not once.

She felt almost crushed by the pressure of his gaze.

'You…can't want to marry me,' she forced out, knowing she had to say something, since it was clear he was waiting for her to do so. 'There must be m-many other—'

'No,' he said, in the same implacable tone with which he appeared to say everything. 'I do not want to marry you. But this isn't about you or me. This is about what is best for Kasimir. I need a queen and you, as an Accorsi, are the most logical choice.'

The tips of her fingers were icy, her chest tight. 'But…but you don't love me.'

The words seemed to echo in the room, the desperate sound of her own voice bouncing off the walls and making her cringe in embarrassment. Why had she said that? What on earth was she thinking? What did love matter anyway?

Of course he didn't love her—not when he'd only just met her.

Love happened in the books she devoured, between people who respected and accepted one another. It happened in real life too, she knew that, but she'd never seen any evidence of it. Her mother had died while she'd been a baby, and it had been made very clear to her, very early on, that neither her father nor her two older brothers had any kind of feelings for her at all.

Beside her, one of the soldiers shifted on his feet as if uncomfortable.

Up on his throne the King stared down at her with an unwavering gaze. His dark winged brows drew down, making her feel all of two inches high as he studied her from the tip of her head down to the soles of her feet and back up again.

'Love?' He said the word as if it was foreign to him. 'This is not about love, *signorina*, this is about duty. All I require from you is your name on a marriage certificate and your presence at my side for official events. Nothing more and nothing less.'

Well, that was something at least, wasn't it?

She'd grown up the only female in a world of men. Selfish, violent men. She'd never had any gentleness, never any kindness and never any care from any of them. To her father she was a nuisance and to her brothers she was prey, to torment and tease and bully whenever they could.

Men were different in books. Some of them were kind and gentle and caring, protective and loving too, so she knew those types of men existed. But not anywhere she would ever meet one—and certainly this king wasn't one of them.

He was probably just like her father. A man who loved power and bending people to his will. Who believed completely that only the strong survived.

She took a little breath. If he was, indeed, that kind of man, then she knew from experience that it was better not to argue. With those kinds of men your only option was rolling over and playing dead. Either that or hiding.

She couldn't hide now, which meant the only thing left was doing what he said.

Still, it was better than the marriage her father had been in the process of arranging for her, to one of his younger advisors. She'd never met him, but if he was anything like her father's other advisors then she knew he'd be awful. They were all awful.

She hadn't had a choice about that either, and all the hiding in the world wouldn't have got her out of it. Her feelings mattered not at all, as her father had so often said. She was only a tool, to be used by him to solidify his support base—nothing more.

However, that *would* have involved more than a mere legal marriage. She would have had to have been in his wife in every way, and the thought of that had left her cold and very afraid.

Give him what he wants. That's your only option.

Yes, it was. And, looking on the bright side, she wouldn't have to sleep with him at least. Then again, what else did he want to do with her bar public events? Would she be his prisoner? Would she be allowed to go anywhere…do anything?

'Th-then what?' she asked, mustering up a courage she hadn't known she possessed. 'How long would the marriage be for?'

His odd light eyes swept over her. 'It will be for as long as I require it to be.'

'But then you'll let me go?' It was tempting fate to keep questioning him and she was appalled at her own temerity. She should just agree to everything and not draw his attention. Yet she couldn't seem to stop herself. She'd been so close to freedom that she couldn't quite let it go. 'Once you don't need me, I mean.'

His gaze narrowed and he continued to stare at her for what felt like yet another eon. 'Are you trying to bargain with me, mouse?'

An unexpected flickering anger caught at her. Angelo and Alessio, her twin brothers, had called her mouse. Because she was small and insignificant and afraid. She'd hated the nickname but never had the courage to protest at it. She'd told herself that she didn't care what they called her, because mice knew how to hide and that was the main thing.

But to have this man, this terrifying enemy, call her the same thing, tarring her with the same brush her brothers had used, rubbed against a place she hadn't realised was raw.

'Don't call me that,' she snapped, before she could think better of it. 'My name in Guinevere.'

Silence crashed down like a lead curtain.

The guards beside her had frozen and Tiberius, up on his throne, was a figure carved from stone.

She'd spoken out of turn. Yet despite her fear, despite the fact that she was his prisoner, she found she didn't want to take it back. She'd rolled over and played dead before with her brothers, who'd used to hunt her through the palace hallways. She'd been traumatised by that as a child—so much so that most of her childhood had been spent in a haze of fear. And now the freedom that had been so close had been snatched away...

Well. She was angry. After years of hoping and praying for an opportunity to leave the palace she'd finally got one—only for him to stop her at the last moment. And not only that he'd accused her of being complicit in her father's actions—whatever they had been—and now he was demanding that she marry him.

It seemed so unfair.

So she didn't take it back. She said nothing as the silence stretched endlessly, clinging to the flickering anger that had sprung to life inside her like a life raft in a stormy sea.

Then, just when it seemed as if it wasn't possible for the tension to stretch any tighter, Tiberius made a dismissive gesture with his hand. 'Leave us,' he ordered.

Almost as one, the assembled guards and other hangers-on turned and left the throne room, their footsteps scuffing on the parquet as they disappeared through the doorway.

Guinevere turned too, a surge of relief making her knees weak.

'Not you,' Tiberius said.

Guinevere watched as the throne room doors shut behind the vanishing guards with a heavy *thunk*, then took a shaken breath and turned back to the throne.

Tiberius had risen to his full height. And then her mouth dried completely as he began to walk down the steps of the dais towards her, stalking her like a tiger stalked a gazelle.

CHAPTER TWO

TIBERIUS WENT DOWN the stairs of the dais towards her, knowing full well that he didn't have time for idle chatter with an Accorsi. Yet that little show of spirit she'd displayed just before had intrigued him, especially given how white-faced and shaking she'd been only minutes before.

He'd been hoping to give the command for the marriage to go ahead immediately, since the priest was already at hand, but a quick discussion with her privately seemed to be in order. He didn't want to put yet another potential Accorsi tyrant on the Queen's throne, so it would pay to do at least a little due diligence on the kind of woman he intended to marry.

He couldn't believe she'd actually snapped at him.

No one had ever dared take that tone with him—not for many years—and yet this little woman…this apparently terrified little woman…had somehow mustered up the courage to chastise the man who'd just taken back his throne for calling her a mouse.

Interesting.

He preferred women with spirit and backbone—in a queen both were vital—and it appeared that, despite appearances, Guinevere Accorsi seemed to have at least a hint of both. That was promising. After all, it wouldn't do for her to be as pale and trembling in front of the public as she'd been in front of him.

Her big blue eyes widened as he approached, her cheeks ashen. There was dust in her hair and on her dress, and a smear of it across one pale cheekbone. That must have come from the secret corridors she'd been scurrying around in, which wouldn't do. His queen shouldn't look like Miss Havisham waiting in vain for her lover. He would have to instruct her not to go into them again.

Tiberius stopped in front of her. The top of her head only came up to his chest so he had to look down. She really was very small and delicately built, gazing up at him from beneath long, pale lashes. It wasn't a flirtatious look. It was more like a deer staring at a wolf with wide, frightened eyes.

Weren't you supposed not *to be threatening to innocent women?*

He wasn't being threatening. And she wasn't innocent—not the daughter of Renzo Accorsi. She'd grown up here. She must be aware of what kind of person her father was, and how badly he'd mismanaged Kasimir. And who was to say that she wasn't the same? Or at least cut from the same cloth? Her twin brothers certainly were, by all accounts.

'I will not hurt you,' he said, just so she was clear. 'I sent my guards away so we can talk without an audience.'

This did not seem to make any difference to the fear in her eyes. 'T-talk about what?'

'About your suitability as my queen.' He gave her another considering glance. 'And also about showing proper respect for the King, especially in front of my guards.'

That glimpse of spirit he'd seen just before, when she'd snapped at him, glowed like blue embers once again. But all she said was, 'Oh.'

The contrast between her fear and her defiance was fascinating. Was it really bravery? Because, if so, that was an admirable quality in a queen.

'They do not like Accorsis,' he said mildly. 'So it would be as well not to give them any excuse to dislike you even more.'

Her sharp little chin lifted. 'I won't apologise. I don't like being called a mouse.'

Something shifted inside him like the earth settling after an earthquake. A certain...interest. She was his captive, and she was afraid, and surely the most logical thing for her to do now would be to ingratiate herself with him. That was what he was expecting—especially from a cowardly Accorsi.

Yet here she was, doing the opposite.

'A simple *No, Your Majesty, I am not trying to bargain with you* would have sufficed,' he murmured. 'What is it about a mouse you find so distasteful?'

She glanced down at her hands, as if the pressure of his gaze was too much. 'I just don't like it. It implies something small and insignificant and...a-afraid.'

Interesting that she didn't like that...despite the fact that she *was* afraid.

'Yet mice can scare human beings,' he said. 'They

can also cause a lot of damage—which is why they are also thought of as pests.'

She kept her gaze on her hands. 'I…am not a pest,' she said finally, the words emphatic.

A silence fell again, and he let it sit there, because silence could be a useful tool. But, unlike most people, she didn't rush to fill it with meaningless chatter. Instead, she gripped her pale hands together even tighter and stared fixedly down at the floor.

'Then what are you?' he asked.

She gave a little shrug. 'No one important.'

He frowned. She'd said the words without any inflection, as if being unimportant wasn't a bad thing, and perhaps it wasn't. The Accorsis had a cruel streak—he knew that for a fact. His mother had died in the coup they'd staged to oust his father Giancarlo. He had been forced to leave his critically injured wife in favour of getting his baby son to safety. She'd been shot by a guard, and the Accorsis had left her to bleed to death in one of the palace hallways. They'd then sent word to his father that that would be his fate if he ever tried to reclaim the throne.

Then there was the treasury Renzo had drained—funnelling money into offshore accounts and into the military, into casinos and palaces and other buildings that no one needed or wanted, while hospitals and schools were forced to operate on less and less every year. Then there were the tax breaks for the rich, and some kind of grand plan to turn Kasimir into a tax haven, which would only be of benefit to his cronies.

A morally bankrupt, corrupt man. And, from the intelligence he'd received, the Accorsi sons had taken on their father's moral compass. Maybe that was true of her too.

Perhaps she'd wanted to be important to them and never had been.

Or perhaps she's lying through her teeth in an attempt to get close to you and assassinate you?

No, that wasn't it. The fear in her eyes had been real, and he'd seen enough of it in his life to know when it was being manufactured and when it wasn't.

She *was* truly afraid. And yet she also had courage enough to snap at him.

Curiosity caught at him along with the urge to test her courage and her fear, to see how deep they both ran. Because he had to know if he was going to make her queen. She would be merely a figurehead, it was true, but she would need to project an illusion of strength at the very least.

He moved closer. 'You were bargaining with me,' he said. 'Weren't you?'

She shook her head, still staring at the floor.

No, he needed to look into her eyes, see what was going on inside her head. He needed to see that courage again. So he reached out and put a finger under her chin, urging her head up.

Her breath caught audibly as her gaze lifted to his, revealing the deep, endless blue of her eyes.

They were beautiful, those eyes. He'd never seen a colour like it. The sky at twilight, blue darkening into a deeper, almost violet blue, so startling in her pale face. Fear was there—he could see it—but also something else. A flickering anger and a stubborn defiance that seemed to reach inside him and grip a piece of him tight.

Such stark contrasts. He found them fascinating. In fact, he wanted to explore them further, with her skin warm and very soft beneath his fingertip, her blue gaze pinned to his.

'Weren't you?' he repeated softly.

Her blue gaze darkened and he was conscious of the sweet smell of jasmine and something more delicate and feminine that made his body suddenly tight.

It had been months since he'd had a woman—not since he'd put into motion his carefully laid plans for re-taking the throne. He hadn't wanted the distraction. He didn't want it now—and certainly not with an Accorsi. But pulling away would be an admission of something he didn't want to admit.

So he stood there, his finger beneath her chin, looking down into her eyes, willing her to reply.

She stayed where she was, though there was still tension in her. 'I'll marry you,' she said at last, her clear voice husky-sounding. 'I will serve my sentence. But at the end of it you will let me go. You will let me leave Kasimir for good.'

Interesting. So she wanted to leave the country? Was it to follow her father and brothers? Because they'd left her behind?

'Making demands in your position is quite the choice,' he said, even as a part of him noted the shape of her mouth and the full pout of her bottom lip. 'You are a prisoner, Guinevere. And after what your father did to this country you should be glad I'm giving you a choice of cell.'

The flicker in her eyes looked like anger, and this time she didn't look away. 'I'm not making demands. I…was going to leave Kasimir. That's all I was intending to do.'

Was that the truth? It seemed to be. Those words, softly spoken with a kind of quiet dignity, weren't something a liar would say, he was sure.

Yet still he couldn't help but ask, 'Why? To go after your family?'

'No. What I want is to escape them.'

Surprise echoed through him. This was the truth. He could see it in those luminous eyes of hers. He wanted to ask her why—wanted to know what had they done to her to send her hiding in the walls where he'd discovered her—but that would be a waste of time. He didn't need to know her. All he needed was her to be his queen.

With an effort of will that was greater than he would have liked, he took his finger from beneath her chin and stepped back.

'Well,' he said, 'I can see no reason to keep you here any longer than necessary. I can't say how long our marriage will be, but once Kasimir is more settled we will divorce and you may leave. But not until then—understand?'

She didn't look relieved or pleased, her skin still pale. 'And I'll be a prisoner until then?'

Irritation wound through him—partly at himself, for being curious and starting this pointless conversation in the first place, and partly at her, for asking annoying questions.

The decision to marry her had been an opportunistic one and he hadn't had time to think through the implications of it yet—let alone what he would do with her outside official appearances. She wasn't as important as the work of surveying the damage Renzo had done to Kasimir and putting in place plans to fix it. He didn't want to waste time thinking about what to do with an unwanted wife.

'We will discuss that later,' he said dismissively, turning towards the doors. 'I will call the priest in. He can perform the ceremony now.'

Her eyes went wide. 'Now?'

Tiberius paused and lifted a brow. 'Of course, now. There is vital work to be done, and the sooner we are married, the sooner I can start fixing my country.'

'But... But—'

'Need I remind you that your father is responsible for nearly destroying Kasimir? If you want to make up for that, may I suggest no more protests?'

She stared at him for a second, with what looked like bewilderment on her face, then she bent her gaze back down at the floor, whatever spirit that had burned in her before now gone.

'Very well,' she said colourlessly.

For some reason that only increased his irritation, though he couldn't imagine why. Yes, courage and strength were important in a queen, but if she didn't have them, then she didn't have them. He didn't need to fight her. He was tired of fighting anyway. Now was the time for peace and the chance to rebuild.

His country would always be more important than his curiosity about one little Accorsi woman.

Annoyed with himself, he turned and strode to the closed doors of the throne room, throwing them open. His guards and aides were on the other side, waiting patiently for him.

'Father Domingo,' he said curtly. 'You are required.' Then he glanced at his guards. 'I need witnesses. You and you.'

The ceremony commenced at the foot of the throne and was over in approximately five minutes. The rings would come later, as would the licence, but such things were insignificant details. What was important was the marriage certificate and her signature on it.

Guinevere was silent throughout, except when she was required to speak, and then she was as good as her word and didn't protest. But she didn't look at him either, keeping her gaze firmly downcast.

He couldn't have said why that needled at him. Why it made him want to put out a hand, grip her chin once more and have her look at him. See exactly what she was feeling in this moment. Whether it was fear or anger or something else…

But no, he didn't need to see it. This wasn't about her, anyway, nor even about him either. This was about Kasimir, and doing what he needed to for the good of his country, and that was the only thing that mattered.

Besides, he wasn't going to force her into doing anything she didn't want to do—not beyond having her signature on the marriage certificate. He wouldn't touch her, and they'd only meet for official engagements. She wouldn't find marriage to him…onerous.

As the ceremony finished, Tiberius turned to his new wife. 'Tomorrow we will speak of the details,' he said. 'Tonight I will have my staff ensure you're comfortable.'

There was nothing more to say, and he had a day's important work ahead of him, so before she could speak he turned around and strode out of the throne room, followed by his men.

Guinevere felt almost in a daze as a guard led her through the corridors following the wedding ceremony.

Somehow, she was married.

Somehow, she was a queen.

It was almost inconceivable that the day she'd thought she'd escape the palace and Kasimir for good, instead she'd found herself trapped yet again.

Trapped first by her name and then by his.

Trapped by a crown and by the ring he'd told her he'd get for her later.

She didn't know how the whole thing had happened so fast, or what she'd done to have fate imprison her so completely like this. It was wrong. Even the concession she'd managed to get from him—that he'd let her go once he had no more need of her—didn't feel like one.

But really, the wedding wasn't even the worst part of what had happened in the throne room. The worst part had been when he'd stalked down that dais and come close to her, and then had put a finger beneath her chin and tilted her head back.

He'd seemed so tall to her, and so broad, overshadowing her like an oak tree, and she'd been expecting cold fear to run through her the way it always had whenever she'd caught the notice of her father and brothers.

Except this time it hadn't. The touch of his finger on her skin had felt scorching, creating an odd tension inside her that had fear as one of its components, yet also something else. Something…more. A kind of anticipatory excitement that had made her skin feel tight and her heartbeat sound loud in her ears.

The intensity she'd seen in his silvery eyes as he'd looked at her had called to a part of her she hadn't realised was even there, and abruptly she'd become very, very aware of him. Of not just his height, or the broad width of his shoulders, but the gleam of the crown against his black hair. The curve of his bottom lip. The stretch of his army fatigues over his muscled chest. The warmth of him, so at odds with those icy eyes, and the scent of him—something fresh and outdoorsy, reminding her of the sun and the sea and the wind that blew between them.

She didn't understand why his nearness had felt that way, because by rights she should have been terrified.

Perhaps she was getting braver.

Or perhaps you were just stupid.

Guinevere thrust the thought away and all her strange feelings with it. They didn't matter anyway—not when he'd made it clear that the only times she'd see him was for public appearances. That was a *good* thing. The less she saw of him the better.

The walk back through the winding palace corridors wasn't easy. They were horribly familiar, these corridors. She'd been walking them all her life and she hated every inch of them. They were a both a maze and a prison, marking the boundaries of the small, insignificant life she'd had within these walls. A prison she'd thought she'd be free of today, and yet—

No, there was no point thinking about that. One day she'd get out of here. Eventually, she would.

She swallowed, shaking her hands to ease the tension that drew tighter and tighter the more they walked. Because she was starting to understand where she was being taken, and every cell of her being rebelled.

'My room is down there,' she said tentatively to the guard as they passed by a branch in the hallway.

'I was not instructed to take you to your room,' the guard answered, without even looking at her.

'But all my things are there and—'

'I was instructed to take you to the royal apartments,' the guard said without inflection, making it clear that he was going to follow those instructions come hell or high water.

Guinevere swallowed again, her throat closing.

The royal apartments. Where her father had lived. Where her brothers had once hunted her down and where she'd hidden, almost wetting herself with fear.

That same fear seemed to grip her now, her breath catching, her fingertips going numb. She hadn't had a panic attack for months, but today she had clearly pushed things too far—because she felt close to one now.

She tried to ignore the feeling as the guard stopped

outside the big double doors that led to the royal apartments, yet the fear kept on rising, swamping her.

The guard pulled the doors open and waited, making it clear she was expected to walk inside.

Dread slid through her like a fine sliver of glass, cold and cutting. She wanted to tell the guard that she couldn't possibly stay here, that she needed to go to her own room, but there was no give in the man's expression.

Come on, pull yourself together. It's just a room. Also, there is an escape, don't forget.

Yes, there was. She didn't have to stay if she didn't want to. And also her father was gone, and so were her brothers. There was no one left to frighten her any more.

No one except the King. Your husband.

Guinevere shoved that particular reality aside and forced herself to cross the threshold, walking through the doors into the private receiving room beyond.

This room wasn't as much of a mess as the throne room, but there were signs of a hurried tidy-up. A mound of what looked like shattered pottery in one corner. A priceless Persian silk rug in front of the fireplace stained. There were a few pictures missing, also, and in one place the panelling on the walls had been kicked in.

The doors shut heavily behind her, then the lock clicked, and no matter how much she tried to resist it panic closed cold, sharp talons around her throat.

Oh, God, they were locking her in.

Breathing fast, she whirled around and went to the door, rattling at the handle and of course not getting anywhere because the guard had turned the key.

'You don't need to lock it,' she called through the door, trying not to let her voice shake. 'I—I promise I won't leave. Please. Just…don't lock it.'

'Sorry.' The guard's voice was unapologetic and flat. 'His Majesty's orders.'

A scream rose in her throat, but she fought it down hard. That wouldn't help, she knew, and it would only make her panic worse. And as for the guard—well, no one had ever listened to her screams, so why would he?

But you're the Queen now, remember?

Was she, though? She didn't feel like one. She had a feeling that if she gave an order the guard would only laugh in her face, and she wouldn't blame him.

Closing her eyes, Guinevere rested her forehead against the door, her palms pressed flat to the wood on either side of her. She took a couple of deep breaths, trying to calm herself.

It was only a room. Just a room.

After a moment, her heart still hammering in her ears, she pushed herself away from the door and turned around.

The room was just as it had been, and yet she could also see the past laid over it like a palimpsest.

Over there was the doorway to the bedroom that her mother had used when she was alive. Once Guinevere had been at a curious stage about her, and had wanted to see what was inside, but she'd been found by her father, who'd ripped her away from the door and flung her onto the floor in a rage. He'd screamed at her never to go near that room on pain of a sound thrashing. She'd been six.

Her brothers had known she wasn't allowed to go

into the Queen's rooms and so of course they'd tried to chase her there, hunting her down in the palace hallways like dogs after a fox. They were years older than she was, and bigger, and they'd been cruel. Her father had done nothing to stop their bullying of her because she was 'only a girl'.

He'd wanted another son, not a tiny, delicate daughter, and when she'd come to him weeping, after having her hair pulled, or her dresses ruined, or her knees skinned after they'd pushed her over, he'd only told her to stop being a 'fraidy cat' and said that if she didn't want to be bullied she had to stand up to them. But she'd tried to do that once and had been given a black eye for her trouble.

She'd tried very hard after that not put herself at risk of being hunted, but for her brothers it had been their favourite game. They'd liked ruining things that were precious to her—especially any hints of prettiness and femininity. They'd thought pouring oil on her favourite dress was a joke, as was tearing pages out of her favourite books. Once, they'd crept into her bedroom at night when she was ten and fast asleep and cut off all her hair.

She hadn't been able to escape them and no one had done anything to protect her. Sometimes she'd wondered what her life would have been like if her mother had still been alive, and whether her mother would have protected her. But it had been pointless thinking about that. Her mother was dead and being frightened of her brothers all the time had been her constant state of being. Yet some small part of her had refused to be beaten, and so even though her pretty dresses and long, curly hair marked her out for more bullying she'd worn them anyway in a show of defiance.

That hadn't helped her, though.

The only thing that had was finding the secret passageways in the walls. No one knew they were there—certainly her brothers didn't. So when it had got bad she'd simply disappeared into them, finding her way to other hiding places around the palace.

Life had become more bearable then, and although her brothers had tried relentlessly to find out how she managed to disappear, they never had. And after a few years, as they'd grown into men, they'd stopped looking and eventually forgotten about her entirely.

Guinevere took another breath, and then another, willing the fear to go away. Because she wasn't in danger now and there was nothing that could hurt her.

But the panic wouldn't go away, and the knowledge that she was trapped here, the way she'd been trapped in this palace for so many years, began to close in on her.

Staying in these rooms was impossible, the weight of her memories and the terror sitting on her shoulders crushing, and there was only one way to deal with that.

Breathing deeply, Guinevere went into her mother's rooms and into the dressing room where the big carved armoire was. She went over to it and pulled open the doors, then stepped inside.

It was always difficult entering the secret passageways through the armoire, because the only reason she'd found them in the first place had been because she'd taken refuge in the armoire one day when her brothers had been chasing her.

They'd worked out quickly where she was and had locked the door of the armoire, telling her they were going to tell their father where she was and he'd give her a thrashing.

She'd become panicky and had kicked at the back of the armoire, since kicking at the door had failed to open it. The back had turned out to be not solid wood but thin veneer, and her foot had gone straight through it into...nothing.

After she'd kicked more of the veneer away she'd seen that there was a narrow doorway in the wall behind the armoire, and an even narrower pitch-black corridor. The darkness had scared her, but anything was better than being shut in the armoire and waiting for her father to find her, so she hadn't thought twice.

She'd escaped into the corridor beyond.

She did so now, even as the fear continued to lap at her, squeezing her chest and throat, making her feel as if she was suffocating.

Then she was through the armoire and into the safety of the darkness beyond.

It wasn't Narnia, but it was an escape, nevertheless.

Guinevere walked silently down the corridor, turned to the left and continued to walk until she came to the end of it. The darkness didn't bother her now, and she didn't need light to find her way around—not when she knew every inch of these corridors like the back of her hand.

A small lever pulled aside part of the wall and she stepped through the opening and into her favourite place in the whole palace: a tiny, forgotten room that no one knew about except her.

It was a small library, with bookshelves and a fireplace, an ancient, uncomfortable sofa and a deep window seat with a curtain over it that one could pull across and be shielded from anyone who might glance into the room.

Guinevere pulled another lever so that the bookshelf that had slid aside to open the doorway slid back into place. Then she went across to the window seat. Over the years she'd gathered lots of blankets and pillows, and other pretty little things, taking them into the little library, turning the window seat into an extremely comfortable bed where she could sleep or read or do anything else, hidden from everyone.

Safe.

She crawled into it now, making sure the curtain was drawn across so no one would see her, then curled up under a blanket and did what she always did when she couldn't escape her fear.

She fell asleep.

CHAPTER THREE

THE DAY AFTER his somewhat casual coronation Tiberius expected to start the morning with a meeting involving all his advisors, who would then help him with the important work of sorting out the mess Renzo Accorsi had made of Tiberius's kingdom.

What Tiberius did not expect was to be informed that his brand-new wife and queen was missing. That somehow she'd managed to get out of the royal apartments—which had been locked—and had apparently vanished into thin air.

It put him in a foul temper—not helped by the fact that he hadn't slept well the previous night. He never slept all that much as it was, but last night his sleeplessness had been entirely due to his body plaguing him with inappropriate urges. For some reason the little mouse had ignited something within him and he didn't like it one bit.

Clearly neglecting his sexual needs had been a mistake which now had to be fixed. The fact that he was a married man was of no consequence. The union was purely political, and he was sure Guinevere wouldn't have a problem with him satisfying his hunger elsewhere. He had no intention of remaining celibate.

So what he wanted this morning was to start work, then perhaps in the evening find a willing woman to deal with his other needs—not to search the palace for a missing Accorsi.

After their marriage the afternoon before he'd spent the rest of the day and the evening sorting through a game plan for his country, then drafting a public announcement of his marriage with his press secretary, including a date for their first royal appearance. However, there couldn't be a royal appearance if he was missing a royal, so find her he must. If she'd somehow managed to escape the palace entirely, then time was of the essence.

Whether he liked it or not, her presence was needed. She was now a vital emblem of unity, the final piece in the strong foundation he hoped to rebuild Kasimir upon, and he wasn't going to let her escape like the rest of her cowardly family.

Deciding to inspect the royal apartments himself, since apparently his men couldn't keep one small woman from straying, he strode in, his temper vile. But after a close survey of each room he realised he couldn't fault his guards. There did, indeed, appear to be no way for Guinevere Accorsi to have escaped, yet the fact remained that she had.

He stood for a long moment in the Queen's empty bedroom, thinking about how she could have got out. Then it hit him—something he should have thought about before and hadn't because he'd been too busy focusing on other things.

The secret passageways. That was the only way she could have got out of this room unseen, which must mean that there was an entrance to them in the royal apartments somewhere.

Tiberius reviewed the floor plans in his head, piecing together a map of the palace and the corridors in order to determine the most likely place for a secret entrance. Then he started methodically looking around for anything that might give away a secret door.

It didn't take him long. A cursory examination of a huge, ornate wooden armoire revealed a kicked-in panel at the back which led into a gap in the wall behind it. He stepped into the gap and the darkness beyond without hesitation.

He wasn't claustrophobic—which was a good thing, because the corridor was a narrow fit and pitch-black. He didn't find the lack of light a problem either. He'd been in worse situations when he'd been in the military, after all.

A couple of minutes later he came to a branching of the corridor, but after a pause to consult his memorised plans he was pretty sure one branch led to the throne room—and surely she wouldn't have gone there, not when it was full of cleaning staff—so he took the one leading in the opposite direction.

Soon the corridor came to a dead end, but feeling around in the dark, he soon found a lever that must open a door. He pulled it—clearly it had been in recent use, since the mechanism moved smoothly—and the wall in front of him slid aside, dim light spilling into the narrow corridor.

He stepped through the doorway and found himself in a small room—a library from the looks of things. There were bookshelves stuffed full of books, an old couch sitting before a fireplace, magazines and a book of crossword puzzles discarded on the cushions. A jug of wilted flowers was on the mantelpiece, along with a glittering pile of what looked like jewellery, a few crystal bottles of perfume and a silver-backed hairbrush.

He frowned, noting the signs of feminine occupation, and yet not seeing the little Accorsi anywhere. Then he noticed the curtains drawn across the window—odd, because it was morning—so he went over and pulled them aside.

A deep window seat lay behind them, and curled up on it, in a nest of blankets and pillows, was his new wife.

She was asleep, her hands tucked beneath her cheek, her curly blonde hair lying in tangles all over the cushions. The morning sun spread like liquid gold over her, bathing her in a kind of glow, and despite himself he felt his breath catch.

So. She hadn't left after all. Likely there had been too many guards for her to escape the palace entirely, so she'd found a place to hide. Maybe she'd been waiting for a better opportunity to escape and had fallen asleep before she could.

Her sleep looked to be deep, and there were faint dark circles under her eyes. In fact, if he hadn't known better, he would have said it was the sleep of someone exhausted.

She was wearing the same clothes as she had the day before. The same dusty white lacy dress. And even the streak of dust across one cheekbone was still there. She clearly hadn't bothered to wash.

Why not? Had something driven her from the royal apartments? And why had she come here? Why had she curled up like a cat and gone to sleep?

He stared at her, the curiosity he'd felt the previous day pulling tight once more and deepening.

She was an Accorsi, from the same family that had put Kasimir through hell and destroyed his own family, and yet curled up on the cushions, small and pale, she had an innocence to her, a fragility that belied her family's history. It tugged at something long-forgotten inside him, reminding him of being very young, long before his father had told him who he was and what his destiny was to be. When he too had been innocent, and all that had concerned him was who he was going to play with at school and whether his father would cook something he liked for dinner.

Was it peaceful, this sleep? And if it was, what would it be like to sleep so deeply that not even the presence of another person standing close could wake you? Long years as a soldier had made him all too aware of the threat of deep sleep, and even now, after he'd left his military career, he didn't sleep well. There were too many things to think about, too many things to do.

Sleeping was a waste of time that he only tolerated in order to keep himself physically well. And he needed the strength to keep moving forward, to keep fighting—because the battle was constant. He couldn't put down his burdens, his duty to his country, not even for a moment.

His mother had sacrificed too much, and if he was

going to deserve the gift of life that she'd given him, then he had to keep going no matter how tired he was.

She deserved better.

Kasimir deserved better.

He had no idea how his new wife could sleep so deeply, given what her father had done, but she must feel safe, here in this little room, to give herself over to sleep like that. He was a little jealous of that. Sometimes there were days when all he wanted to do was lay down those burdens. To rest. To sleep as Guinevere Accorsi was sleeping, deeply and without fear.

He should wake her, not stand there staring at her, and yet he didn't move. Because he was becoming aware of other things. Things he should not be aware of. Such as how the blanket was half falling off her and how her dress was pulled up, revealing one gently rounded thigh. And the way she was lying made the neckline of her dress gape slightly, giving him a view of the soft darkness between her sweetly curved breasts.

A pretty little thing…

Almost without conscious thought, he let his hand come out to touch the dusty streak across her cheek—perhaps to wipe it away or maybe just to feel the texture of her skin. He wasn't sure. But bare inches from her face he stopped.

His hands were soldier's hands, scarred from missions and battles and roughened from long hours spent training, and he had the oddest thought that if his fingertips brushed her cheek he might harm her. That he might mark her pale skin like the rough point of a nail against sheer silk.

Does that matter? She is an Accorsi. You could touch her...have her. Corrupt her as her family corrupted Kasimir. That would be an apt vengeance.

His body had gone tight, his breath catching hard in his throat.

No, those weren't thoughts worthy of a king. He didn't thirst for vengeance for his mother's death, no matter how many times his father had told him he should. He was a protector, and he protected his subjects. And, Accorsi or not, she was one of those subjects. Corrupting her would end up making him no better than her father and he would not do that.

He would *never* do that.

Besides, regardless that their marriage was only political, she was his wife and his queen, and that made her worthy of his respect.

Tiberius straightened, bringing his recalcitrant body back under ruthless control, and opened his mouth to give her a curt command to wake up.

However, before he could get the words out her silvery lashes fluttered and her eyes opened. She looked up at him, the deep, dark blue of her eyes holding him captive, and her mouth curved in an unexpected welcoming smile, as if he was a friend and she was delighted to see him.

His heart caught hard inside him. No one had ever looked at him the way she was looking at him right now. His army saw a general they were loyal to, his aides a king they must obey. It was always awe and fear and respect—never happiness. Never delight. He hadn't known he'd wanted that until this moment.

Then she blinked a couple of times and her eyes went wide, as if she was only now processing the fact that he was here. Abruptly she sat up, rearing back against the window seat, the smile disappearing, her face going pale with unmistakable terror.

And that caught him too—like the bite of a whip.

She was scared of him.

Are you surprised, when you forced her to marry you? She was scared of you yesterday too.

Disappointment gripped him, though he told himself he didn't feel it. She was right to be scared. She was an Accorsi and she should fear him. Marrying her wasn't quite the vengeance his father wanted, but in a small way it was to punish Renzo. He would certainly not be happy to learn that his daughter had married his enemy.

'Good morning, my queen,' Tiberius said flatly.

'Wh-What are you doing here?' she asked in a shocked voice. 'How did you find me?'

He folded his arms, his mood fraying. 'It wasn't difficult. The door to the royal apartments was locked, and yet you'd disappeared, so I assumed you'd vanished into the secret corridors again.' He glared at her. 'It seems I was correct. And now you have wasted my guards' time and mine by vanishing without a word.'

'I'm sorry.' She remained pale, eyeing him warily. 'I didn't want to stay in the royal apartments. I have my own room in the palace. I did tell the guard that, but he said your orders were to put me in my parents' rooms. I didn't know he was going to lock me in there.' She lifted a hand and pushed the mass of golden curls off her face. 'I would have told someone where I was going, but there was no one around to tell.'

'This isn't a hotel, Signorina Accorsi,' he said severely. 'You cannot pick and choose your rooms. You are the Queen and your place is in the royal apartments.'

She glanced down at her hands, now twisting in her lap the way she'd done the day before in the throne room.

It annoyed him. Did she think that he'd hurt her? That he was the type of man who would raise a fist to someone much more vulnerable than he was?

Preposterous. He was a king, not a bully, and the only people he'd ever hurt physically had been other soldiers during fighting. Never a civilian. Still less a woman.

'I'm not going to hurt you,' he snapped. 'You needn't act like a beaten dog.'

Her shoulders hunched, as if his tone had physically hurt her—which, for reasons he couldn't articulate, only annoyed him further.

'I never would have thought that an Accorsi would protest at being given their due,' he went on. 'You should be grateful I decided to put you here and not in a prison cell.'

She shook her head, but said nothing.

He didn't know why this incensed him. 'Well?' he demanded. 'Give me one good reason why I shouldn't put you in a cell right now.'

Guinevere's heart was beating far too fast and far too hard. The muzzy, sleepy feeling she'd woken up with was long gone, washed away by an icy flood of fear.

She'd been having a lovely dream… She couldn't

remember quite what it had been about, but she knew she'd been safe, and it had been years since she'd felt that way. But then she'd woken up to find a very tall man standing beside her window seat, glittering grey eyes looking down her. Her first thought hadn't been one of fear. Only that somehow it was right he should be standing there—that in another life, or in another dream, she knew him, and while he was there nothing bad could get her. She was safe.

Then her brain had kicked into gear and she'd processed exactly who it was standing by her window seat. And the fact that she wasn't safe. She wasn't safe at all.

A burst of adrenaline had hit her then, making her sit bolt-upright and lean back, pressing herself against the window in order to get away from him.

Tiberius. The King. And he was angry.

It was always bad when a man was angry. Always.

He wasn't in fatigues today, nor was he wearing a crown, but he might as well have been, given the aura of power rolling off him.

He was dressed simply and all in black. Black trousers and a perfectly tailored black business shirt, no tie. A lesser man might have looked like a monk, or even a waiter, but no monk or waiter had ever radiated such crackling electricity. It seemed to wind around her and grip her by the throat, making her mouth go dry.

The morning sun was shining full in his face, making his grey eyes glitter like icicles, his black hair glossy as a raven's wing, highlighting his strong nose and the shape of his mouth, the hard lines of his jaw…

She didn't understand why she was noting all this

about him, or why she was thinking that 'handsome' was too conventional a word for this man and didn't quite encompass the sheer charisma of his physical presence.

She didn't understand why she felt almost stunned by it, or why she had to look away from him just so her brain would work.

What was happening to her? Why did he have this effect on her? She should be afraid of him—and she was—but that was starting to fade now, especially since she couldn't stop looking at him. It was as if he was a tiger about to take a bite out of her and all she could think about was the beauty of his fur.

You know why. You might be sheltered, but you're not stupid.

Guinevere swallowed. She'd read all about physical attraction. It was there in her favourite books. But she'd never felt it herself. Never met a man who made her feel anything at all apart from afraid. Until now.

It made no sense. He was clearly angry with her—which he had a right to be, she supposed, since she had disappeared without telling him. But still... She hated confrontation, especially when men got into a rage, because when they did, people got hurt. And he was so much larger and stronger than she was...

Yet despite all that her heart was beating fast and her skin felt tight, and she wanted to keep looking at him because he was also beautiful to her.

Your husband.

There was something flat and so final in the word 'husband', and it made her shiver. She had no examples of what a husband was—none at all. Her father never spoke about her mother, so what he felt about her Guinevere had no idea.

'Well?' Tiberius demanded, his deep voice shattering her thoughts and somehow getting under her skin.

What had he said? Something about this not being a hotel and wasting his time and being a beaten dog? Oh, yes, and jail cells. And he was angry.

He came into your safe place without asking and now he's demanding yet more things from you. How dare he?

A small thread of anger began to wind through the cold grip of fear—because, yes, how dare he come in here, demanding explanations from her? Calling her names and threatening her? This was her private space—*hers*.

'I'm sorry,' she forced out, staring at her hands and ignoring her anger.

Getting angry only made things worse. Apologies, even if you didn't mean them, were the best thing for calming angry men. Then again, they'd never worked on her brothers—not when her very existence had made them torment her.

'That's all?' The edge in his tone rubbed against the same raw place it had rubbed against the day before. 'You're sorry?'

She knew it was always a mistake to fight back against someone more powerful than you, and yet that small thread of anger grew hotter, brighter, and abruptly she was sick of him. Sick of his demands and sick of her own weakness at caving in to them.

A beaten dog, he'd called her, with contempt in his

tone. And of course he'd be contemptuous. He was tall and strong and physically powerful. He was King.

He'd probably never lived in fear of being hurt or maybe even killed by those who were supposed to love you and protect you. He wouldn't know what it was like to be small and fragile and utterly defenceless. He wouldn't know what it felt like to be hunted like prey.

How dared he judge her when he knew nothing whatsoever about her? How *dared* he?

'Well?' she snapped before she could stop herself, looking up and meeting his silvery, icy gaze. 'What else do you want? I apologised.'

He was standing there, towering over her, muscular arms folded across his broad chest. Obdurate as a mountain.

'You have wasted my time, mouse,' he said flatly. 'I have a country to fix and I do not want to spend the entirety of my morning running around after an Accorsi.'

Beaten dog. Mouse. Small. Insignificant. Powerless.

If he had been either of her brothers she would have cowered, sick with fear. Yet for some reason, just like it had the day before, her anger only flickered higher, hotter, making her lift her chin in unconscious insolence.

'Then don't. No one asked you to run around after me.'

His eyes widened a fraction and she thought she caught a glimpse of surprise there. Clearly he hadn't been expecting her snap back at him. Well, good. She *wasn't* a beaten dog, and she was tired of being treated like one.

He'd said he wouldn't hurt her, and maybe he'd been

telling the truth, but right now she didn't care. She didn't have any energy left for fear.

'I don't like the royal apartments,' she went on, since she might as well while she had the courage. 'There are bad memories there. So if you don't want me to have a panic attack, I suggest that you don't lock me in any more and either let me stay in my old room or here.'

'A panic attack?' he repeated slowly, his black brows drawing down.

'Yes. I presume you know what they are?' She gripped the edge of her blanket, her anger burning higher and hotter at the unfairness of it all. At how he'd had her locked into a place full of past trauma and then been angry with her for trying to leave it. At how he saw her—vulnerable and frightened—and found that contemptible.

'But maybe you don't,' she went on hotly. 'Since you're the King now. And kings don't ever have panic attacks, do they? They never get scared and they're contemptuous of those who do. They never stop to think about the poor dog, or even of why it was beaten in the first place.'

The torrent of words fell into the silence of the room, echoing around her, and immediately she knew she shouldn't have said anything. She shouldn't have confronted him. She should have bowed her head and kept on apologising, kept on appeasing him, done whatever he'd ordered her to do. Because talking back drew attention and attention was never a good thing. It only made everything worse.

Except it was too late. She'd been pushed one too

many times, and this man, this enemy of hers with his disturbing presence, who'd made her marry him and talked sternly of prison cells and beaten dogs, had been the last straw.

She might be small and defenceless, but she'd found some unexpected steel inside her—so too bad if he didn't like what she'd said.

His face was impassive, his gaze sharp, betraying nothing of what he thought about her tirade. But she lifted her chin even higher, just to show him that she didn't care what he thought. Didn't care that she'd snapped at him and wasn't showing him the respect he'd spoken about the day before. Not a bit.

What could he do to her anyway? Put her in a prison cell? She'd been living in one for all twenty-three years of her life, and nothing could be worse than this palace. Nothing.

He was silent for a very long moment. Then he said, 'For a mouse, you have quite sharp teeth.'

'Don't call me that,' she said fiercely. 'I am *not* a mouse. Or a damn dog!'

His gaze glittered, focusing on her with disturbing intensity. 'No,' he murmured. 'Clearly not.'

A curious prickling sensation swept over her skin in response, making it feel tight and hot, as if his icy silver gaze was akin to a physical touch, and a flush of heat crept up her neck and into her cheeks, warming her.

She was blushing and she didn't know why—and it only made her angrier. The way he was looking at her, his irritation with her, and the dismissive way he'd spoken to her kept rubbing against that sore spot, fraying nerves already frayed from what had happened the day before.

She'd been so close to getting away…so very close. But he'd caught her. He'd dragged her from the safety of the shadows and into the light, making her his prisoner, making her marry him, trapping her yet again in this hateful place. And now he was getting angry with her because she'd wasted his time.

All of a sudden she hated him. Hated his silvery gaze and the way it made her feel. Hated the way he called her mouse. And most of all she hated how he assumed she was pathetic and cowardly—and she wasn't.

'And stop looking at me that way,' she said angrily, shoving herself off the window seat, pleased when he took a couple of steps back to give her room. 'You hateful… hateful b-bastard.'

He said nothing, merely tilted his head to look down at her, assessing. And she stared back, all the blood in her veins hot with a fury that had been there all her life, waiting in the shadows like her. But now it was out, bursting its banks like a flood tide, and for the first time since she could remember she felt powerful. She felt strong.

Perhaps if her brothers had been here she wouldn't have cowered.

Maybe she would have punched them in the face.

'No, not a mouse at all,' he said slowly. 'What would you prefer to be, then?'

'Why not try my actual name?'

The look in his eyes shifted, became sharp-edged as an icicle. It moved over her slowly, as if he was taking her in, cataloguing her every feature, and it made her suddenly breathless.

Then he said, his dark, deep voice lingering on each syllable, 'Guinevere.'

A shiver crept over her skin and she nearly trembled. He'd said her name like a poem, or a song, and so slowly—as if he was tasting it, taking his time over it.

She'd never heard anyone say it like that. Mostly because no one had said it at all. She was always and for ever either 'girl' or just 'mouse'.

She stared up at him, her anger slowly ebbing away. It felt as if he'd given her an unexpected gift and now she didn't know what to say.

The morning sun slid over his night-dark hair, shining full in his face, making his odd light eyes look crystalline, the planes and angles of his features highlighted with exquisite perfection.

She was standing very close to him, she realised then, as close as she had been yesterday, in the throne room, when he'd put his finger beneath her chin. And she felt again what she'd felt back then. The warmth of his body and his scent, an intoxicating mix of sun, salt and warm earth. It made her imagine the wind in her hair, walking in a summer forest, maybe, or on a boat, riding the waves.

Freedom. He smelled like freedom.

Breathing felt difficult, and every thought went out of her head as the air around them became weighted with a tension she didn't understand. Her cheeks burned and her heartbeat sounded far too loud. And in place of her anger was something else. Something hotter and more demanding.

He had gone very still, that intensity back in his eyes.

If she lifted her hand, she could touch him. She wouldn't have to reach far, since there was barely any distance between them. What would he feel like if she did? If she laid her hand on his chest? Would he be as hard as she imagined? Would he feel as hot? What would he do if she did?

She felt dizzy at the thought, and breathless too, as if she'd run a long way and very fast.

What are you doing?

She had no idea. She had no idea why she even felt this way. And yet she felt consumed by it. By him.

An eon seemed to pass. All the air in the little library was vanishing, bit by bit, and she knew it had something to do with him—with his height and the broad width of his shoulders and that glitter in his eyes, which weren't quite as icy as they had been. No, if she wasn't much mistaken, it looked as if there were silver flames burning there instead.

Then, quite abruptly, he turned away. 'I have no time this morning to discuss our marriage,' he said in curt tones. 'It will have to be this evening. I will send for you.'

Then, before she could say another word, he stalked out.

CHAPTER FOUR

TIBERIUS PACED BEFORE the fireplace in his office, restless, impatient and vaguely out of sorts. He'd spent all day in meetings with his aides and advisors, sorting through the difficult task of imposing a new government upon a nation that had been under martial rule for the last twenty years.

A parliament needed to be reinstated and elections held—because he had no intention of holding on to power. He was no dictator. Then budgets needed to be looked at and press releases drafted. And naturally there was the issue of a public appearance.

He needed to do that as quickly as possible, so that his people would be reassured that Kasimir was once more being governed by someone responsible. There had been reports of unrest, which he'd expected, but that only made him even more impatient to get to the task of delivering reassurance to his subjects.

There weren't enough hours in the day…that was the problem.

He came to the end of the long silken rug that lay on the parquet before the fireplace, turned around, and paced back to the other end of it.

There were other things that needed to be done too. Such as the clearing up of the palace. The King's office hadn't been vandalised, as the other rooms had, and it hadn't taken more than half an hour for a couple of the palace cleaning staff to get it in order. Just as well. He needed a place to work with no distractions.

The room held an antique carved oak desk, a fireplace, oak bookshelves standing against the walls, and had a huge window behind the desk that looked out over the crags of the mountains that surrounded Kasimir.

A utilitarian room, with very little in the way of frills, but it suited his soldier's temperament.

He came to the other end of the rug, turned, and paced back once more.

Then there was the other question. The one he'd been trying not to think about all day and yet had pushed to the front of his thoughts far more often than he'd wanted it to.

The little Accorsi. The mouse who was clearly not a mouse—as she'd demonstrated so admirably this morning.

He couldn't stop thinking about the unexpected fury in her eyes when he'd confronted her about escaping. Or about how she'd shoved herself off the window seat to stand before him, curls spilling everywhere, dust on her cheek and anger blazing in her deep blue eyes.

Panic attacks, she'd said. Bad memories, she'd said. That was why she'd escaped from the royal apartments and into the hidden corridors.

Tiberius turned once more and paced another circuit in front of the fire.

Then the look in her eyes had changed...blue becoming violet as something hot and electric had arced between them.

She hadn't been a beaten dog or a mouse then.

She'd been a woman.

He gritted his teeth, his muscles tightening once more in response to the memory.

Yes, he couldn't deny it. The way she'd stood up to him, the way she'd blazed defiance at him and then the way her eyes had darkened had been...exciting. It had been obvious to him that she'd felt the same electricity, and with her standing so close, all spirit and fire, he'd had the almost overwhelming urge to take that sharp little chin in one hand and cover her mouth with his, taste all that fire for himself.

You could. She's your wife. You could make her yours in every way. You could make her want you...crave you. Put her on her knees before you. That would be a fitting revenge for what the Accorsis did to your country...

A growl escaped him as all the blood in his body rushed below his belt. Yes, Renzo Accorsi's forgotten daughter on her knees, naked before him... She'd have all those pretty curls loose, giving him something to hold on to as he defiled all that innocence, all that sweetness—

No. *No.* Why was he thinking of this again? He'd dismissed those base thoughts this morning, back in that little library, so why they should be returning again he had no idea.

He wasn't that type of man. He was a king. And a

king didn't indulge in anything as petty as revenge—still less with some innocent.

Perhaps she's not innocent?

Perhaps so. But still their marriage was for Kasimir only, and that did not involve anything physical. Besides, he preferred women less fragile, women who liked their sex hard and rough, and the little Accorsi was definitely not a hard and rough type of woman. She'd mentioned panic attacks, for God's sake, and she'd certainly been terrified of him, which rendered her immediately off-limits.

So no, even if she hadn't been an Accorsi he wouldn't have touched her.

And as for this…chemistry. Well, he'd ignore it. Physical attraction was easy to control—and besides, if it proved too distracting he'd find himself one of those women who liked it rough. It didn't need to be his new wife.

Speaking of…

He stopped pacing for a moment and glanced at his watch. He'd sent her a message earlier that afternoon, instructing her to present herself in his office at six p.m. sharp. Dinner would be served and they would discuss their little…arrangement.

It was now five minutes past six and she was not here.

His restlessness intensified, eating at him, and he broke from his pacing, headed over to the door, intending to go and find her. He pulled it open only to see her standing on the other side of the doorway, her hand raised to knock.

Her eyes widened, her mouth opened, and much to

his annoyance he found himself staring at it. Because it was a pretty mouth. He could think of many things he could do with that mouth…

Another growl almost escaped him at his own way-ward thoughts, but he managed to wrestle them into submission.

Guinevere was not in the same dusty lacy dress she'd worn this morning, but a light blue one, with lots of frothy tiered skirts that made her look as if she had a fountain falling down on either side of her. She had her hair tied back, curls cascading down her back in a more orderly fashion than it had been this morning, and the dust on her cheekbone had gone.

She still looked delicate, like a fairy, if a much more tidy one than she had the previous day, and despite the control he had himself under he found his gaze coming to rest on the neckline of her dress, which was low and scooped, providing a perfect showcase for the swell of her breasts.

She will be soft. How long has it been since you've had any softness?

Too long. His life had been nothing but hard, relent-less action, always moving forward, always onwards to the next plan, the next strategy. There had been no time for rest, for anything gentle or light or soft.

There was still no time for it.

And he should *not* be thinking about this as con-stantly as he was.

Forcing his gaze away from the neckline of her dress, Tiberius stepped back from the doorway. 'You're late,' he said tersely.

She blinked. 'By five minutes.'

'Five minutes is time enough for someone to lose their life.'

'Really? I had no idea this meeting was a matter of life and death.'

Acid laced her words as she stepped into the room. So. It seemed the little mouse was definitely a thing of the past.

He shouldn't respond. She knew nothing about what he'd gone through to get here and it wasn't worth arguing about. That didn't stop the words from coming out of his mouth, however.

'You have no idea about many things, Guinevere Accorsi, and that is why you are here—so I can discuss them with you.'

Hot blue flames leapt in her eyes, turning her once more into the fiery, spirited woman who'd stood up to him in the library that morning. The polar opposite to the quiet, terrified girl who'd kept staring at her hands, too afraid to look at him.

Maybe she isn't as fragile as you thought.

He did not need that thought in his head. No, he most certainly did not. Because now he was intrigued by the contrast, and by how, for all her delicacy and fragility, there appeared to be a fire burning in her. A fire he found fascinating.

She put her chin in the air and moved past him, going over to the chair in front of his desk and sitting herself down in it like the little Queen she was. 'Well, then, Your Majesty,' she said. 'Here I am.'

Tiberius shut the door and walked over to the fireplace, where he'd been pacing not moments before. He stopped, folding his arms as he looked at her.

She had her hands once again clasped in her lap, but for a change she wasn't looking at them. She was looking at him, anger still leaping and flickering in her deep blue eyes.

This evening she was a lioness, perhaps. A lioness in a pretty blue dress...

'First,' he began, starting with his most pressing concern, 'I cannot have you disappearing again. The entirety of the palace was in an uproar this morning, because you'd decided to vanish without warning.'

'I told you why I did,' she said hotly. 'I told you that I—'

'Yes, yes,' he interrupted, impatient. 'However, you must understand that I've only recently taken power, and there is still unrest in this country. I married you to end division and create stability, and you vanishing without a word significantly undermines that.'

She glowered at him, her pretty mouth tight.

'You do understand that, don't you?' he demanded insistently. 'Or does the wellbeing of our country not matter to you?'

All at once her hands came out of her lap and she gripped the arms of her chair, shoving herself out of it in a furious movement. 'Of course it matters to me!' Her voice was so fierce it shook slightly. 'But I didn't know what was happening. I wasn't ever allowed to leave the palace, and all my father said about the state of Kasimir was that everyone loved him as King.'

Her vehemence took him by surprise, and for a moment he only stared at her. What did she mean, she hadn't been allowed to leave the palace? And did she really not know what Renzo had done to Kasimir? How could she not?

Guinevere stood in front of her chair, fingers clenched into fists at her sides, her cheeks pink, fury blazing in her eyes.

He'd hit a nerve, that was clear, and in that moment a cold awareness swept over him. That fury wasn't fake or manufactured. It was the truth.

Her father really *had* never let her out of the palace. And perhaps she really *hadn't* known what was happening in Kasimir either. But how could that be?

The awareness deepened into shock. He forced it back. Renzo was a monster, but she was a grown woman. She must have had some inkling about what kind of ruler her father was.

You say that like you expected her to have stopped him, somehow, or done something about it.

Perhaps. He needed to know more—and not just for himself, but for Kasimir. He needed to know if the woman he'd married so abruptly was indeed the right Queen for his country. Possibly it was something he should have questioned her more thoroughly on the day before, but it was too late to regret that now.

'I'm not accusing you of anything,' he said coolly. 'That's not what I was saying.'

She was still trembling with emotion. 'Then what were you saying?'

His first instinct was not to be comforting. He had no experience of it. He was a leader, a commander, a soldier. A man of quick, decisive action. He left the job of reassurance and comfort to others more skilled in giving it than he was.

Yet it was clear that Guinevere needed more than decisive action, and since there was no one else around to reassure or give comfort, his would have to suffice.

Pushing his impatience aside, he took a step towards her, then stopped and gestured to the chair. 'Sit,' he said, in what he hoped was a gentle tone, though it came out sounding more like an order than he'd wished. 'Please,' he added.

Her chin was jutting at a stubborn angle, but after a moment she let out a breath, unclenched her hands and sat back down again.

'This is about Kasimir,' he said. 'The short answer is that your father mismanaged the treasury, spent too much money on palaces and monuments and not enough on infrastructure or on basic social services. The country is in a terrible state, and it is my job to rebuild what he almost destroyed.'

She glanced away, her shoulders hunching, as if what he'd said was another attack.

'Marrying you is part of that,' he went on. 'As I told you yesterday, there are still deep divisions within Kasimir and people still sympathetic to your father. I want to unify this country, heal those wounds, and our marriage is a potent symbol of that healing.'

Again, she said nothing, her head bent, her gaze on her hands, and before he knew what he was doing, he'd come over to her chair and reached out, taking one of her hands in his. He had no idea what prompted the urge to touch her. It hadn't ever occurred to him before to touch another person in comfort.

She didn't pull away, and because her fingers were cold he began to rub them gently with his thumb. 'I should not have implied that the wellbeing of our country was of no importance to you,' he allowed. 'Especially when I don't know anything about your life.'

Now her gaze was fixed on her hand in his, and he became conscious that her skin had warmed. It felt smooth and silky beneath the brush of his thumb. A familiar electric awareness swept through him, tightening his muscles, and he wondered if she was as smooth and silky all over…whether that faint, sweetly feminine scent that surrounded him was her hair or her body or a combination of the two.

Not that he should be thinking about her body. He should not be thinking such thoughts at all. And he definitely should *not* be touching her.

With an effort of will that cost him far more than it should, Tiberius let go of her hand and stepped back, ignoring how the warmth of her skin lingered on his fingertips.

'I think you need to tell me, Guinevere,' he said. 'About what your life was like here.'

Guinevere could still feel the warmth of his hand around hers. His skin had been so hot, and there had been a slight roughness to the pad of his thumb as he'd stroked it over the back of her hand.

It had been unexpected, and she'd had to steel herself not to flinch, since the last touch she'd had from anyone male—her brother Alessio—had involved a chunk of her hair being torn out.

But there had been nothing violent about the way Tiberius had taken her hand within his. Nothing rough about the gentle chafe of his thumb. The feel of it had sent the most delicious shivers down her spine.

She couldn't think when he was near her...her thoughts getting as slow and heavy as thick treacle.

That afternoon, because of a couple of things Tiberius had said, she'd found one of his aides and pestered him into telling her what her father had done to Kasimir. He'd always boasted about the good things he'd done for the country, and how his subjects loved him, and while she'd doubted that—because she'd certainly never loved him—she hadn't seen anything to the contrary and hadn't been able to get any information from anyone.

Finding out the truth had been like a sliver of glass in her heart. It had made her feel dreadful, and complicit in some way, even though she'd had no choice about her imprisonment. And then Tiberius accusing her of knowing what had gone on and not doing anything about it had shoved that sliver even deeper.

It had hurt, his accusation. But it had been his admission of regret for the way he'd spoken to her that had taken the wind completely out of her sails. No one had ever apologised to her for anything. Not her brothers for their treatment of her, and certainly not her father.

For Tiberius to reach out and touch her had further shocked her. Not so much the fact that he'd done it as her own reaction to it. Being touched with gentleness was a new experience for her, and there had been something infinitely warm and reassuring about his hand around hers. A big hand, and scarred, yet it had held hers carefully, as if it were precious.

She hadn't known men could be capable of gentleness. Her father hadn't been, for example, and neither had either of her brothers. They'd taken pleasure in having power over others, as if cruelty were a kind of strength, and they'd encouraged it in the guards they had surrounded themselves with too.

Guinevere had spent all day anticipating this meeting and not in a good way—especially after hearing what had happened to Kasimir. She'd known Tiberius would be angry, and that he might be accusatory, and so she'd dreaded facing him.

But part of her knew that she had to face up to what her father had done, even though it wasn't her fault, so she'd showered and changed into one of her favourite dresses to give herself courage. And then she'd forced herself to meet him here in the King's study.

He had been angry and accusatory, as she'd known he would be, but what had surprised her was the anger that he'd woken in her that morning had once again ignited, roaring up inside her like a bonfire.

She should have kept it locked down and away, because arguing and making a scene drew attention to herself, and that had never ended well for her, but she hadn't been able to control it. She'd expected him to retaliate in kind—because men like him always did. Except...

He hadn't.

Instead, he'd apologised and taken her hand in his, asked her to tell him about her life.

She had no idea how to respond.

He'd let go of her now, and was standing back, putting distance between them, his back to the fireplace, silver eyes betraying nothing. But she could still feel the brush of his thumb scorching her skin. Why had he done that? Was it because he felt sorry for her?

She was tempted to ask him, but then decided she didn't want to know. She didn't want any sympathy—and definitely no pity. She'd ignore it, pretend it hadn't happened. That seemed the safest route.

'There isn't much to tell,' she said. 'I was born here and grew up here. I was educated here too, along with my brothers. But… I wasn't allowed to leave the palace. My father told me it was because he was concerned for my safety.'

Tiberius's dark brows drew down. 'Even when you were older?'

'My brothers were allowed out, but not me. I was a…a girl. And I was to be protected.'

Except there had been no protection from the monsters within the palace walls. She'd had to protect herself, because there had been no one else. But she didn't want to tell him that. He'd only pity her even more and she couldn't bear it.

She didn't know what he thought about her imprisonment. He gave no sign. His features were impassive.

'And you truly didn't know anything about what was happening in Kasimir while your father was in power?'

There was no accusation in his voice this time, only a note of puzzlement—as if he couldn't quite conceive that she hadn't known.

Well, he could believe what he liked. She knew the truth of her childhood.

'No,' she said flatly. 'I didn't. The only thing I was told was that Kasimir was returned to its former glory and that everyone loved the King. I wasn't allowed electronic communications until I was eighteen, and even then my access to the web was tightly controlled.'

He was still frowning. 'You must have heard rumours...'

Guinevere let out a breath, thinking about the whispers she'd overheard while hiding in the passageways. Whispers from the staff, from the guards, from guests. Whispers about the state of the economy and joblessness, about the statue that had gone up in one of the city's central piazzas that had cost millions—money the country could ill afford to spend.

It had struck fear into her heart, listening to them, because it had sounded so awful. And because there had been nothing she could do to help. She was only one small mouse in the walls, whom everyone had forgotten.

'I heard things,' she admitted. 'Once I tried to talk to my father about it, but he told me that it wasn't my business and to stay out of it. So... There was nothing I could do.' Tearing her gaze from the flat expression in Tiberius's eyes, she glanced down at her hands yet again, acid collecting in her stomach. 'So, I suppose you're right, in a way. I was complicit in my father's crimes.'

A silence fell over the room.

She could feel him looking at her—judging her, no doubt. And he had a right to. Her father *had* almost ruined Kasimir, while all she'd been worried about was her own safety. She wasn't any better than he was. Because she too had fled and hid.

'How did you know about the passageways?' His tone was impossible to read. 'My father used to tell me stories about them, but he said no one else knew about them.'

She didn't want to tell him the truth—that she'd merely been a toy her brothers had used to hone their bullying skills on, and that instead of standing up to them she'd hidden in the walls. She could only imagine what he would think of that. He was tall and strong and powerful. He wouldn't understand fear. He would think her a coward, just like her father, and he'd be right.

'I discovered them when I was playing hide and seek with my brothers.' It wasn't exactly a lie…merely a variation of the truth. 'The armoire in my mother's rooms was locked, and I couldn't get out, so I kicked open the back of it and found the opening behind.'

'The lock is on the outside of the armoire doors,' he said, his tone expressionless. 'It would require someone to actually turn the key to lock you in.'

Guinevere swallowed and looked down at her hands, twisted in her lap. She didn't want to tell him. Didn't want that icy silver gaze to judge her the way he judged her father.

'I don't know how that happened,' she said carefully.

There was a silence.

'I think you do.' His voice was soft, but there was something hard and unyielding in his tone.

In spite of herself, Guinevere glanced up. The expression on his face now was frightening in its intensity, his silver eyes sharp as knives, and even though she knew that he likely wouldn't hurt her, she couldn't help her instinctive flinch.

'What did they do to you?' he asked, in the same unyielding tone. 'And they definitely did something. I can see it in your eyes.'

There was no judgment in his face, but there was certainly anger, and she wondered why. What did he care what had happened to her? No one else had.

You should tell him the truth.

She didn't want to, but it was clear he suspected what the truth was, and she had a feeling he wasn't going to let her leave until he had it. And, really, what did his judgement matter anyway? Yes, he was her husband, but it wasn't as if they loved each other—not when they'd only just met.

'My father didn't touch me,' she said, choosing her words carefully. 'But my brothers liked to…tease me.'

The hard glitter in Tiberius's gaze didn't falter, but a muscle leapt in the side of his strong jaw. 'How? By locking you in the armoire?'

'Yes,' she admitted.

'Were there other things they did?'

Her mouth was dry, but she forced herself to speak. 'They liked to…chase me through the palace. And pull my hair. Sometimes, when I was much younger, they'd break my toys.' The look on his face had changed, and now it frightened her. 'It wasn't anything too bad,' she added quickly.

'Did they hurt you?'

'Please…' she said without thinking. 'Please, don't be angry.'

His eyes widened for a moment, as if what she'd said had surprised him, before narrowing into glittering silver slits as he studied her. 'I'm not angry with you, Guinevere,' he said quietly. 'I am angry with those who hurt you.'

Something inside her eased at that, and she realised she'd been sitting there tensely, as if waiting for him to explode in a furious rage, preparing to run from the room in fright.

He's not going to do that, and you know it.

Perhaps she did know it. He seemed to be in a constant state of annoyance, and yet he did not throw anything or scream obscenities the way her father did, or say cruel things and laugh the way her brothers did.

He was contained, she thought. Self-possessed and impervious. And for some reason that made her feel safe.

'They...did hurt me,' she said in a rush—because he'd asked for the truth and she wanted to give it to him, especially since he'd already guessed. 'That's why I hid in the passageways. So they wouldn't find me.'

Tiberius's expression remained hard as stone. 'They will pay for it,' he said, pronouncing the words like a vow. 'They will pay for what they did to this country and for what they did to you.'

Surprise rippled through her. 'Why should you care about what they did to me?'

'You are my queen, and as King it is my duty to protect you as I do all my subjects.'

She heard it then. The steel beneath his tone. He stood before the empty fireplace, muscular arms folded, a severe expression on his face and his light grey eyes glittering with intention. A strange kind of thrill went through her. She'd never had anyone state that they would protect her—not one single person. But, looking at his fierce expression, she believed him.

He absolutely *would* protect her.

That made her feel warm, and immensely reassured, and for the first time in what felt like years her muscles relaxed. She let out a breath. 'Thank you,' she said, and she meant it, though she didn't know what else to say— she didn't want to keep talking about her brothers. 'But you didn't ask me here to talk to me about my life. You wanted to discuss our marriage.'

At that moment there was a knock on the door. Tiberius gave her one long, sharp glance, then turned to answer it.

A minute later the room was full of serving staff who unloaded food onto the huge wooden desk that was the only available flat surface in the room. They arranged it along with a bottle of wine from the palace cellars, and then left as discreetly as they'd come.

'I've had dinner brought to us,' Tiberius said. 'The main dining room has yet to be cleaned and, given your feelings about the royal apartments, I thought you would prefer to eat here.'

Another little shock went through her. She hadn't expected him to think about that. She hadn't expected him to think about her feelings at all.

'Thank you,' she repeated, which appeared to be her standard response.

'Eat.' He gestured at the food. 'You must be hungry.'

It was true—she was. She hadn't bothered with lunch.

She'd stayed in the safety of the little library, too out of sorts and uncomfortable with Tiberius's intense electric presence to leave it.

She still felt that he might be a danger to her in some way, but it wasn't the same as the sick dread that used to fill her whenever she heard her brothers' voices. No, his danger felt almost exciting...which was very strange. Anyway, the food was there, and her stomach was empty, so it seemed silly to refuse.

Rising from the chair, she went over and helped herself. It was a simple meal—salad and fresh bread and roasted chicken.

Tiberius poured her a glass of wine as she pulled a chair up to the desk and began to eat.

'There will be some making do until the palace has been fully restored,' he said, pouring a glass for himself too. 'As you can see.'

'I'm sorry,' she felt compelled to say. 'For the condition my father left the palace in.'

'Did you spray paint the walls and burn the tapestries?' he asked mildly.

'No, but—'

'Then you have nothing to apologise for.' His silver gaze was very direct. 'We must present a united front as rulers, Guinevere. I have been thinking on this and I have decided that our marriage must at least look cordial, if not joyful. We will need to be seen together, as well as making official public appearances together. I want our union to look strong and steadfast—do you understand?'

A tight, hot feeling prickled over her skin. 'Strong and steadfast? How?'

'The King's bedroom is part of the royal apartments, which means we will have to share them.'

The prickling feeling deepened. 'Sh-share?'

Tiberius finally picked up his glass of wine, slowly swirling the deep red liquid inside it. 'Not the bedrooms. We'll keep those separate. But we should be seen to retire to the royal apartments together, at least initially, as any newly married couple would.'

Her stomach tightened for reasons she didn't care to examine too closely.

'You don't have to sleep there if you don't wish to,' he continued. 'No one knows about the corridors, which means no one will know if you choose to sleep in that little room.'

The warmth that had been sitting inside her ever since he'd touched her hand and then said he'd protect her deepened. She might be his prisoner, but he was granting her a space that was hers and hers alone, free of the memories that soaked through every other part of the palace. It was almost as if he was taking her feelings into account.

She could feel colour rise into her face, but she didn't look away from him this time. 'You really won't mind?'

'I don't see why not. You shouldn't have to deal with memories that upset you.'

'I…appreciate that.'

He gave her a regal nod in acknowledgement. 'And another thing… You'll need some preparation, I think, before our first public appearance.'

'Preparation? What kind of preparation?'

'You say you haven't ever left the palace. Not once.

But public appearances will involve not only leaving the palace, but visiting various Kasimiran cities. There will also be international engagements we will need to attend.'

An unfamiliar excitement filled her, even as the thought of venturing outside made her nervous. There was embarrassment there, as well, at how sheltered she must seem to him—backward, even. Though why she should feel embarrassed about something she hadn't had a choice in, she didn't know.

'Good,' she said, forcing away the odd mix of feelings. 'That won't be a problem. It's not as if I wanted to spent the last twenty-three years stuck in here.'

His gaze was considering. 'I don't want to throw you into the deep end straight away—especially not with the public looking on. Perhaps we can acclimatise you to the outside world a little before then.'

You'll be going outside. Actually outside!

A quiver ran through her. 'Acclimatise how?'

'We can start somewhere within the palace grounds. The forest...or the orchards, perhaps.'

The orchards she'd seen out the windows of her little room, full of many different fruit trees. Sometimes she'd imagine herself being able to walk amongst the trees, reaching up to pick herself an orange or a peach.

'I was only allowed in the courtyard gardens and on some of the terraces,' she offered hesitantly. 'I haven't been to the orchards or the forest.'

'In that case,' Tiberius said, 'we shall start there.' Then, unexpectedly, a faint smile turned one side of his mouth. 'Now. I was told my new queen didn't touch her lunch today, so eat—please.'

That smile. It turned him from charismatic to utterly beautiful in seconds flat. And it felt to her as if she'd been given a gift…a glimpse of the man behind the hard, stern King. A warmer, easier kind of man.

But then the smile vanished.

As if it had never been.

CHAPTER FIVE

TIBERIUS DIDN'T REALLY have the time to spare to acclimatise his new queen to the outside world. There were too many other, more important things to do. Yet the thought of one of his aides or guards accompanying her on her first venture beyond the palace walls was unacceptable.

He hadn't been able to stop thinking of her sitting in his study the night before, white-faced and delicate, hesitantly telling him that her brothers had hurt her.

He'd known, maybe subconsciously, that something like that must have occurred—especially given her terror of him. But her confession, veiled as it was, had filled him with the most intense rage on her behalf. That anyone had dared lay a hand on her, so fragile as she was, was incomprehensible to him. Though he knew men did such things and worse every day.

That it had been her brothers, her family, who should have protected her and cared for her, made it even more egregious, and he burned to know what they'd done to her and why her father hadn't stopped them. But he'd bitten down on the questions. He hadn't wanted to upset her further with intrusive questions, especially since his knowing wouldn't change anything for her.

But when he'd told her he would protect her he'd meant it. Her brother and her father would pay. And if anyone else laid a hand on her they would answer to him.

Bullying behaviour was unconscionable in royal princes and most definitely in a king, and he would never be like that. Never.

Her first time outside the palace walls would be with him, so he could watch over her—as he should his queen. Also, she would be at his side for their public appearances, and he needed to see how she reacted, so that if she was overwhelmed he'd know what to do and have some solutions. The eyes of the world's press would be on them and, as he'd told her, he wanted their marriage to at least look as if it was solid.

Taking her outside himself would also kill two birds with one stone—he could get her used to being out of the palace and also to being with him. It would not do for her to flinch away if he put an arm around her, for example.

Eventually, a few days after their dinner together in his office, he found a couple of hours free in the late afternoon.

He hadn't seen her since then because he'd been working from dawn till midnight every day, wrestling with the thorny issues of getting his country back on track. The damage the Accorsis had done to the Kasimiran treasury was considerable, though not as bad as he'd expected, so that was something at least.

He sent word to Guinevere to meet him by the doors to the back gardens, and when the hour came he strode down the echoing hallways, expecting to see his queen waiting promptly outside the specified doors. Only she wasn't.

It took him a moment to realise that the tension in his muscles and the accelerated beat of his heart was anticipation.

For the past two days he'd been good, and he hadn't thought about her once. There hadn't been room in his head for her anyway. But late at night, when he finally left his study for bed, he'd come into the royal apartments to find a tantalising sweet scent hanging in the air, one that made his body go tight with want.

He'd ignored it, thinking that hard work and late nights would mean he was too tired to think about his new wife. Sadly, he'd been wrong. That delicate scent would greet him and instantly he'd start to think about her, naked and at his feet—which was a terrible fantasy for him to have about a woman who'd been hurt as she had.

It had frayed his temper, put him on edge, and had helped him with his sleep not at all.

Which meant that by the time Guinevere finally arrived, five minutes after the time he'd specified, his mood was dark and irascible.

That she was in another of her pretty flouncy dresses, this one soft pink, with full skirts and a heart-shaped neckline, only added to his annoyance. Her hair was completely loose, in a cotton-soft cloud around her head and down her back, and he was conscious of an unbearable need to wrap those curls around his fingers and tug lightly. Then maybe not so lightly…

No, that was a mistake. He should not be thinking any of this.

Unlike the previous times they'd talked, when she had been either white-faced with fear or angry, today Guinevere smiled at him as she approached, her deep blue eyes lighting up and something deep inside him stilled.

People smiled at him—of course they did. But not like this. Not as if they were pleased to see him. As if his presence gave them joy.

He was a leader, and his advisors, his guards and his army respected him. Feared him. Admired him. But they never looked at him the way she was looking at him…as if he was simply a man she liked and liked being with.

'I know, I know,' she said as she came towards him. 'I'm late. Sorry. I was trying to find a ribbon for my hair and couldn't, and then…' She trailed off, noticing the scowl on his face.

'I have limited time,' he snapped. 'I do not have it to waste, waiting for you.'

She reddened, her smile fading. 'I said I was sorry.'

The loss of that smile angered him even more. Because he knew he was being unreasonable, that she probably had had enough of men being angry. But knowing he had no one to blame for that except himself only made it worse.

Other people's feelings had never concerned him, and his own he kept under strict control. Emotions were irrelevant, his father had always said. The only thing of any importance was Kasimir and his duty to it, and everything else should come second.

Except right now his sharpness had hurt her, and

he didn't like it that he was the cause. She'd no doubt been hurt enough, and she didn't need him adding to her trauma.

'There is much to be done,' he felt compelled to explain. 'Time is of the essence. The people of Kasimir have suffered enough under your father's rule, and the longer I take to fix the problems, the longer the people will suffer.'

She frowned. 'Surely it's not *all* dependent on you?'

'Of course it is.' He tried to rein in the sharp note in his voice. 'I am the King now. The ultimate responsibility for our people is mine.'

She studied him. 'That seems…an awful lot for one person to bear.'

The observation hit him uncomfortably, though he wasn't sure why. Yes, it *was* a lot for one person to bear. Which was why his father had started early in preparing him for it.

From the age of ten he'd been told what his purpose in life was: to reclaim his father's stolen crown and rescue his country.

His journey to the throne room had been a long and hard one, but he'd survived it. His father had died before he could see Tiberius reclaim what had been lost, but now he was here and had begun the process of rescuing his country. His father's ghost could be at peace now.

And now you can make the Accorsis pay—especially for what was done to her.

No, regardless of how furious he was about that, vengeance was a petty action and he was above it.

'Not for me,' he said shortly. 'I was born to do this.'

Her brow furrowed, as if she found this worrying. 'I... I could help,' she said a little hesitantly. 'If you like.'

His instinctive reaction was to snap that he didn't want help, especially not from an Accorsi, and how could she help him anyway? But he simply couldn't countenance letting his temper get the better of him any more than he had already.

It wasn't her fault that he was letting her get under his skin. The blame lay with him entirely.

'You can help by being at my side as my queen,' he said carefully, impatient with her questions and the unwanted emotions they brought. 'So, are you ready to walk to the orchards?'

'Yes.' Her hands were once again clasped tightly in front of her, which he was beginning to see was a sign of her anxiety. 'I'm not agoraphobic or anything. Just so you know.'

She might not be, but it was clear to him that she was nervous.

'We will take it slowly.' He turned to the big double doors, opening them so they could step out onto the terrace. 'The orchards aren't far.'

He took the lead, stepping through the doors, then turning around to face her.

Guinevere stood still in the doorway, blue eyes slightly wary, the set of her shoulders betraying her nervous tension.

Without thinking, he held out his hand to her. 'Come.'

She reached for it without hesitation, and for some reason that satisfied him. As if her taking his hand meant something. It didn't, of course, he was only trying to reassure her. And yet he didn't let go of it as she stepped through the doors to join him on the terrace, and the satisfaction deepened when, instead of pulling away, she held on tighter.

He met her gaze. 'Are you ready?'

She took a little breath, then nodded, and they began to walk slowly to the end of the terrace and then down the stairs to the path into the gardens. Guinevere's blue eyes were wide and she kept looking around—at the sky, the grass, the gardens, then back at the palace, its towers soaring into the heavens, mirroring the mountain peaks around them.

She was brave, this little mouse of an Accorsi. Despite what had happened to her—which he suspected was a lot worse than she'd said—she had a thread of courage running through her that gave her unexpected steel.

He watched her keenly, alert for signs of fear, yet there were none. Her cheeks had gone pink, the sun was striking golden sparks from her hair, and when she looked at him her smile was full of delight.

'I'm outside,' she said breathlessly, as if she couldn't believe it herself. 'I'm really outside!'

Tiberius hadn't found much to smile about in life— the stakes had always felt too high for levity—but the simple joy on Guinevere's face touched something long-forgotten inside him.

Back when he was boy, before his father had laid the heavy burden of kingship on his shoulders, he'd often gone out into the scrubby garden of his father's rundown house after he should have been in bed. And he'd lie on his back, looking up at the stars. Pinpricks of light against the black background of space. Whole worlds, whole galaxies spinning above his head. He'd felt that simple joy then, at the beauty above him, and a sense of wonder that he too was a tiny part of those galaxies.

He'd forgotten what it felt like to experience joy... to find wonder in such a simple thing as being outside in the sun.

And you *did this for her.* You *gave her this.*

The things he did for his country helped his subjects as a whole, but this was personal. Now he'd given this one woman joy, and it made his heart tighten in a way he wasn't used to.

And it shouldn't—that was the problem. The way she was getting under his skin felt like...more, somehow. Beyond physical. And that was *not* allowed.

His father had told him time and time again that a ruler's feelings didn't matter. That what was good for the country mattered more.

'Patience, Tiberius,' Giancarlo would say sternly, when Tiberius, burning with anger at his mother's death and desperate to put things right, had tried to argue his father into action, instead of waiting, as his father had counselled. 'Kasimir will not be served best by impatience and a desire for vengeance. You must put your feelings aside and do what is right for the country, not what is right for you.'

Emotion had no place in a king's rule and he knew it, and he'd decided long ago that it was easier not to have any at all. Or rather to learn to channel his grief at being deprived of a mother he didn't remember and his anger at a father who had put an impossible burden on his shoulders at far too young an age and then waited too long to take back what was his. All that rage and grief he'd channelled into reclaiming the throne, and now he'd channel those same feelings into rebuilding his country.

There wasn't room for him to be concerned with the emotions of one small woman, no matter how brave she was.

He let her hand go, since she apparently didn't need any reassurance, though it was difficult to keep any distance between them with the warmth of her skin against his fingertips.

'How are you feeling?' he asked.

She frowned, her fingers clenching into a fist, as if she wanted to keep the touch of his skin against hers with her. Then her expression relaxed and she lifted her face to the sky, clearly enjoying the sun on her skin.

'I feel…' she murmured. 'I feel as if I can breathe again.'

He couldn't stop looking at that little fist. Holding on to his warmth.

You affect her.

Tiberius turned away abruptly. He didn't need that thought in his head…he really didn't.

They continued on through the lavish palace gardens where fountains filled the air with a soft music, then went down more stairs and through a small gate. The orchards lay beyond, situated on a sunny slope.

Guinevere made a delighted sound and ran past him, heading straight to the orange trees. They were in season, and the branches were heavy with fruit.

He followed more slowly, watching her. How childish of her…to run like a little girl to the tree. He almost expected her to hike up her dress and start climbing it.

Was that what it was like to have no burdens whatsoever? To be free to enjoy the sun and the grass and the trees without having the weight of other people's expectations on you? Guinevere had her own burdens, it was true, and they were terrible ones, but now it was as if she'd simply shrugged them off and sprung free, weightless in the sun.

Suddenly he burned to know how she did it—how she made it look so easy to just…step away. To lay down the weight of those burdens and spend a few moments without it crushing you down.

He watched her with a kind of wonder as she stood at the base of a tree, reaching up to try and pick one of oranges hanging just out of her reach. Even on her tiptoes, with her hand outstretched, she couldn't reach it.

She turned then, her face alight. 'This might sound crazy, but I could see these trees from the window of my room. And I used to have this fantasy of being able to go outside and pick an orange if I wanted to.' She glanced back up at the fruit above her. 'So now I'm here, I'd really like to pick that orange. Could you give me a boost?'

The request was so out of left field it took him a few moments to understand. 'You…you want me to lift you up?'

She'd gone up on her tiptoes again, reaching up to touch the orange hanging from the branch above her, laughing at little as she tried and failed to touch it. 'Yes, please.'

He didn't think it through. He moved over to where

she stood, coming to stand in front of her. Then he put his hands on her hips and lifted her so she could pick the orange.

And it was only once she was in his arms, the warmth of her body pressed to his, the sweet, feminine scent of her curling around him, that he realised his mistake. Because it *was* a mistake. She felt soft...so very soft... and he'd almost forgotten what soft felt like. His life had been hard and from a young age he'd been driven, his father forging him like a blade on the anvil of hardship, of struggle.

He hadn't missed gentleness, hadn't missed softness, because he'd never known either. But he could feel both in her, and the dark craving inside him deepened, intensified.

'You can put me down now,' Guinevere said breathlessly, holding her fruit and looking down at him with a triumphant expression.

He stared up into her depthless blue eyes, alight with a joy he hadn't thought was still possible. Her cheeks were pink and she was warm against him and he didn't want to put her down. He wanted to keep hold of her, feel that warmth and softness against him for a little longer, even though he knew he shouldn't.

Reluctantly he lowered her, doing so slowly, because he couldn't help himself, easing her down the length of his body so her pretty curves pressed against his...the giving swell of her breasts and hips in his hands, the softness of her thighs sliding down over his.

Her eyes widened, the blue deepening into the most fascinating violet, a blush rose beneath her skin and her lips parted. At the base of her throat he could see the beat of her pulse, hard and fast. She was still clutching her orange, but she wasn't looking at it. She was looking at him as if mesmerised.

Had she liked the feel of him as much as he'd liked the feel of her?

For a second neither of them spoke, then her gaze dipped to his mouth and an arrow of pure desire punched him hard in the stomach, stealing his breath. He should step back, let her go, put some distance between them. But the way she was looking at him was intoxicating.

She wants you. You know she does.

He released her hips and took the orange from her hands. 'Here,' he murmured. 'Let me.'

And he began to peel it slowly.

She didn't make any effort to step back, remaining where she was, standing close, with barely an inch between them, watching him peel the orange.

It was dangerous to have her so close, to do what he was intending, yet he couldn't stop. And once he'd finished with the peel and discarded it onto the grass he pulled apart the fruit, holding a segment between his fingers.

'Open your mouth,' he ordered softly, letting her see what was in his eyes, making no secret of the desire that tightened every muscle in his body.

This was a challenge—that was all. A test of his own control. He had no doubt he would pass it. He only wanted to see what would happen if he made it clear that he could feel this electricity between them. He wanted to know what she'd do. In his head he'd already pictured

her blushing deeply and stumbling back—because, after
all, her interactions with men hadn't been pleasant ones.

But she didn't.

Instead she opened her mouth, her gaze fixed on his.

Desire flared bright inside him, and before he knew
what he was doing he'd lifted the segment of orange to
her mouth and her small white teeth were taking a bite
out of it. She chewed and swallowed and then took the
rest of segment from his fingers, the softness of her
mouth brushing against his skin, followed by the touch
of her tongue as she licked the juice from his thumb.

An electric shock arced straight through him, stealing his breath, stealing all thought. And then, obeying
an urge he couldn't have resisted if he'd tried, he took
her chin in a firm grip and bent his head to taste the
sweetness of her mouth.

Guinevere knew he was going to kiss her. She could feel
it…could see the intention laid bare in his silver eyes.
Perhaps it had been a mistake to get him to lift her up
so she could pick the orange, but she hadn't been thinking straight. She'd just wanted to pick the fruit. Then,
as he'd eased her down the length of his body until she
was on her feet again, she hadn't been thinking at all.

There had been only him and the granite press of
his chest against her sensitive breasts. The hard feel of
his thighs. The heat of his skin and the smell of him,
salt and sea and dry earth, now overlaid with a musky,
masculine scent that made her mouth go dry with a new
and painful desire.

When he'd taken the orange from her and begun to

peel it she hadn't been able to drag her gaze away from the movement of his hands. Long, blunt fingers…scars on his skin. Large, rough hands and yet gentle enough remove the peel without tearing the delicate skin of the orange itself.

The contrasts in him fascinated her.

Her heart had begun to beat loudly in her head, prickles of heat sweeping over her. She'd known that it was a mistake to stay so close to him, but she hadn't been able to bring herself to move away. And then, when he'd offered her the orange segment, she'd seen desire in his intense grey gaze, a flame burning, and along with it a challenge.

She wasn't sure what had possessed her to obey his order and open her mouth, but she hadn't been able to stop herself. Maybe it was the sudden surge of bravery that had swept over her as she'd stepped out of the palace and into the gardens, her hand in his. Or the delight of having the sun on her face and the wind in her hair, the rich scent of the forest and the slight tinge of snow on the mountains.

It had all been thrilling, amazing, and for the first time in her life she hadn't felt afraid—not of anything.

She wasn't afraid of him either. Nor of the blatant heat in his eyes.

That was thrilling too, and a deep part of her was flooded with a sudden sense of power. That this warrior, this enemy, this king, should look at her like that. Her, the forgotten mouse hiding in the walls of the palace. The girl no one had ever cared about enough to protect, or even just not to hurt.

He wanted her.

And, while she'd never known what it was to want anyone physically before, she *was* certain that right now she wanted him. Honestly, why wouldn't she? He was dangerous, but so beautiful, and even though that should have made her feel threatened, it didn't.

He would never hurt her. She knew it the way she knew her own name.

He was in dark suit trousers today, with a deep blue shirt that made his eyes glow blue-silver, standing out starkly against his olive skin. He'd been terse when she'd arrived late, explaining to her with some severity exactly what his issue with time was. She hadn't expected that. She hadn't expected, either, the rush of sympathy she'd felt when he'd told her that he was responsible for his country. It had seemed like such a heavy burden, and she'd told him so. But he'd shrugged it away.

Then he'd held out his hand to her to help her step outside, despite the glower on his compelling features, and she hadn't even thought why that might not be a good idea, she'd just taken it.

He was a severe man, vibrating with a taut, impatient energy she found absolutely mesmerising. His hand was warm, and so was his body. And when she'd bitten through that segment, and the juice had run down his thumb, she hadn't been able to stop herself from licking it, tasting the sweetness of the orange and the salt on his skin.

She could taste those same things now, with his mouth on hers...oranges and salt and something darker, richer. Delicious. He smelled like freedom and tasted of courage, and she wanted those two things more than she wanted her next breath.

Thought was difficult, and his kiss was hot, and she could barely take in anything else. Then the kiss turned even hotter, became demanding, and she couldn't resist opening her mouth beneath his.

He took advantage, his tongue exploring hers, making her tremble all over.

Somehow her hands were pressed to his chest and she could finally feel the hard muscle beneath the cotton of his shirt. She'd had no idea he would feel so wonderful. No idea that the rough demand of his kiss would be so incredible.

His fingertips holding her chin tightened and she felt his other hand slide to the small of her back, the orange falling unnoticed on the ground. His hand slid further down, over her rear, cupping her, easing her hips against his, and the hard length of his erection pressed to the unbearably sensitive place between her thighs.

A helpless whimper escaped her as a shock of pleasure sent sparks along every nerve-ending. She'd had no idea it would feel like this. She'd imagined it—yes, she had. Kisses. Touches. Desire. This was what she'd read about. *This*. This magical feeling of being wanted and of wanting herself. But it was better than she'd ever imagined…so much better.

The kiss turned feverish and he released her chin, sliding one hand into her hair and closing his fingers into a fist, tugging back her head, exploring her mouth deeper and with even more demand. She was shaking now, and the hard press of him between her thighs was almost unbearable. She wanted his hand there—wanted something more… More friction. Yes. She needed it.

He moved, walking her insistently backwards until she felt the rough trunk of the orange tree pressed against her spine, his hands on her hips holding her against it. Then he tore his mouth from hers and she found herself looking up into his face, half dizzy with desire and breathing fast. He was breathing fast too, the look in his eyes blazing with want, and with something else that looked like fury.

'Is this what you want?' he demanded suddenly. 'To debase yourself with me?'

Guinevere blinked up at him, not understanding. 'Wh-what do you mean…debase myself?'

'You want me to have you up against this tree? Your skirt hiked up and me inside you? Because I will, little Accorsi. Say the word and that's exactly what will happen.'

She stared at him, noting the hard lines of his face and the anger—yes, it *was* anger—flaming in his eyes. 'I… I…' she stammered, hating how she couldn't get the words out. 'Wh-what did I do?'

'Nothing. But I like it rough, mouse.' He growled the words, pressing his hips suddenly against hers, letting her feel the hard length of him through her dress. 'And you don't even know what you're doing when you look at me that way.'

Guinevere's pulse pounded in her ears, her cheeks burning. She still didn't understand his anger. 'What way?'

'Like all you want me to do is put you on your back in the grass, spread your thighs and eat you alive.'

The words sent a hot shock through her. She knew what he was talking about—she might be sheltered, but she'd read enough about physical passion to understand. The thought of him doing that to her excited her, thrilled her, even as it made her want to go up in flames with embarrassment.

She took a shuddering breath. 'But... I don't understand. Would that be wrong? Why are you so angry?'

Abruptly, Tiberius shoved himself away, then pushed a distracted hand through his black hair, glancing away, a muscle leaping in the side of his strong jaw. Then he looked back, his gaze a silver spear piercing her right through. 'I have never had a problem with controlling myself, Guinevere Accorsi. Never. Doing my duty to Kasimir is the most important task I can conceive of and I should be thinking about it—not of ripping your clothes off.'

Her mouth opened, but no sound came out.

'I don't know why, or what it is about you that is driving me to distraction, but let me be very clear. Nothing can happen between us. I am not the man for a virgin who has lived her entire life within the walls of a palace—and especially not if that virgin is vulnerable, fragile and has been badly treated by the people who were supposed to protect her.'

The way he said it all, so dismissively, caught at something inside her, igniting her own anger. He was acting as if *she* was the problem, and yet she'd done nothing. Nothing at all. It wasn't her fault that her brothers had been monsters, that they'd hurt her. It wasn't her fault her father had failed to protect her, either.

And as for the 'virgin' stuff—well, again, that wasn't her fault. Even if by some miracle she'd met a man she liked, she wouldn't have had the opportunity to rid herself of her virginity anyway.

'Why not?' she shot back, stepping forward. 'You make me sound like a sad little victim, and I'm not.'

The scorching silver of his gaze swept over her. 'No, perhaps not. But the problem isn't you—it's me. I'm afraid of what I want to do to you. I want to punish you, corrupt you, take my revenge out on you for what your father did to my family.' The flames in his eyes were cold now. 'But I am a king, and a king is above such pettiness. He does not put his own desires before those of his country. To do so would make me no better than Renzo, and I will not be that man.'

A shiver passed over her, and she didn't know whether it was because of the ice in his voice or the flames in his eyes.

Punish you...corrupt you...

She swallowed, her mouth dry. 'If you're worried about hurting me, you won't. You would never make me do anything I didn't want.'

She knew that was true. He could have done what he'd just said to her at any point over the past few days and he hadn't. Even when he'd been angry.

His eyes glittered, sharp as swords. 'But I can make you want it, little mouse. I can make you do anything I command. And that's why nothing can ever happen between us.'

'What if I wasn't a virgin? If I was experienced?'

That muscle jumped in the side of his jaw. 'A moot point, since you are neither of those things.'

There was no use in denying it. Her inexperience must be obvious. 'I know that, but...' She tried to think. 'I mean, I'm your wife. So are you planning on being celibate for the entirety of our marriage?'

An emotion she didn't understand flickered over his face and he gave a low, mirthless laugh. 'No. No, I am not.'

A strange feeling lanced through her then—a kind of pain.

You're jealous now?

She wanted to deny it, tell herself that she felt nothing for him so of course it couldn't be jealousy. And yet... The thought of him with someone else made her hurt deep inside. 'You'll...take a lover, then? Is that what you're saying?'

There was a darkness in his eyes now. 'I will not be staying celibate just for you, little lioness.'

Lioness.

Brave as a lion. That was what he meant, wasn't it? He thought she was brave.

She took another step, wanting to prove it both to herself and to him. 'You have made demands of me since we met, and I've given you everything you wanted. I married you. I gave you my name and promised to be at your side for public appearances, for the sake of our people. So you've already punished me for my father's crimes.' The words kept on spilling out, even though she'd had no idea she was going to say them. 'But it's my turn now. I want to demand one thing of you.' She took another step, then another, the last one carrying her straight to him. 'Don't find a lover, Your Majesty. If you want one, your wife is right here.'

His gaze flickered, then blazed with a bright, hot, fierce emotion that again she didn't understand. He was breathing fast, as she was, his hands in fists at his sides.

Was that her effect on him? Had she driven him to this point?

They stared at each other for what felt like one long, aching eon.

Then abruptly he turned around without a word and strode away.

Disappointment gripped her as she watched his tall figure vanish up the path and into the gardens, along with another tight, hot feeling that was almost unbearable.

He might think her brave, but he still thought of her as fragile and vulnerable too, thought that she needed to be protected. She liked it that he wanted to protect her, but she didn't want him to put her in the 'delicate and fragile' box. It aggravated her.

She was tired of being thought of as a victim, of being powerless and weak. Throughout her childhood she'd accepted those labels because it had been safer. But they chafed now. He'd called her a lioness, he thought she was brave, and she wanted to prove that to him—show him that she wasn't as fragile as he thought.

She wanted him, his touch, his kiss. She wanted the passion she'd read about in books and the pleasure too. And she didn't see why she couldn't have it.

Yes, she was inexperienced, and he'd been very clear

about what he liked sexually, but it hadn't frightened her. It had made her curious, made her want to find out exactly what he meant by 'rough'. Because she wasn't some shy, wilting flower—or a bloody mouse.

She took a slow breath, determination hardening inside her.

He wanted her. She excited him—she could see that. But he was also denying himself, because he was a good man, with strong principles, and no matter what he said, he wasn't like her father—not even a little bit.

He would make her want it, he'd said. Well, that was a two-way street. She could make him want it too. Why shouldn't she?

Why shouldn't she, for the first time in her life, actually take what she wanted for herself instead of hiding away in the dark? Also, it wasn't just about her. It was clear he needed what she could offer. In a way, convincing him to sleep with her would be helping her country. A distracted king wasn't ideal, after all, and from the looks of him he needed some relief. He'd been working so hard. She'd seen the shadows beneath his eyes.

Guinevere walked over to where the rest of the orange lay and picked it up. She tore off a segment and put in her mouth, and as she walked back to the palace she began to plan.

CHAPTER SIX

THE REST OF the day was a nightmare. Tiberius threw himself back into the endless list of tasks he had to do, along with all the interminable meetings he had to attend. But it didn't seem to matter how hard he tried to distract himself—and he tried *very* hard—all he could think about was her.

Her mouth. The sweet taste of her. The warmth and softness of her body against his. The unexpected fire in her eyes as she'd told him that she wanted him. That, should he want a lover, she was right there.

His wife. His lovely, lovely wife.

The devil on his shoulder whispered to him all day, giving him good reasons for why he should take her, indulge himself with her. She wanted him. Everyone likely thought they were sleeping together already. And besides, he'd need an heir at some point, and she would be a good candidate to give him one. Also, his concentration was shot, so if he really wanted to put his country first he shouldn't be hesitating.

They were already married, for God's sake, and he wanted her...

He had to resist, though. Because if he could not control his own appetites, how could he put some distance between his rule and that of Renzo Accorsi? How could he do justice to what his father had taught him?

And then there was the way Guinevere had been traumatised by her brothers and by her father. The last thing she needed was a man like him forcing his desires on her.

Even now, he still couldn't believe his behaviour in the orchard, when he hadn't been able to control himself, letting go the leash and gripping her so tightly, holding him to her as if he wanted to cover himself with her softness and sweetness and warmth...

No, he shouldn't be thinking about this. At all.

The meetings went on all day and he was surly to everyone, no matter how hard he tried to keep his temper under control.

He should have found himself a lover, of course, but that was impossible now. He'd told her the truth—that he'd never intended to be celibate—and she'd made her wishes very plain. Now, if he took a lover, not only would it be an admission of weakness he couldn't allow, it would also hurt his new wife, and he didn't want to do that.

How he was going to last until the time came for a divorce, he had no idea...

It was very, very late by the time his last meeting of the day ended and he finally let all his exhausted advisors retire to their beds. Tiberius considered visiting the palace gym, to work off a little of his agitation, but he was tired too, and he'd be useless tomorrow if he didn't get at least one full night of sleep.

He strode through the dark palace hallways to the royal apartments. His guards were the only people still awake. He wouldn't encounter Guinevere, he was certain. She'd have long since gone back down the secret corridors to her little nest in the room where she slept every night.

Sure enough, when he entered the apartments and shut the doors behind him they were dark and silent. He could smell the lingering scent of her, though, all sweet femininity and delicate musk that made his body tighten with want.

Ridiculous to be pushed to the edge by one woman. He couldn't understand it.

In his private bathroom, he pulled off his clothes and showered. Then he towelled himself dry before heading into the darkness of his bedroom.

Only to stop in the doorway, every one of his threat senses going into high alert.

Someone else was in the room, he knew it. And there was that scent again, sweet, feminine...

He stilled for a second, then reached out and hit the light switch.

Kneeling in the centre of his bed, wearing nothing at all, was his queen.

Guinevere.

Blonde curls cascaded over her pale shoulders, the ends caressing the most beautiful pair of rounded breasts he'd ever seen. Soft pink nipples, creamy skin, the delicious curve of her hip and the pale expanse of her thighs. And between them the sweetest little thatch of curls...

His body went instantly hard, every muscle drawn tight.

Her deep blue gaze met his and there was absolutely no fear in it, only sparks of the passionate fire he'd seen earlier that day when he'd kissed her.

'Guinevere,' he said roughly. 'What are you doing? I told you nothing could happen between us.'

She lifted her sharp little chin. 'I've been in the dark for a long time, Tiberius. Hiding in the walls. But I've decided I don't want to do that any more. What I want is my husband. What I want is a wedding night.'

It had been a very long day, and he was tired, and all of a sudden it felt as if he'd been doing nothing but fighting. Fighting for his throne, his crown, his country. Fighting for years without a break. And fighting himself most of all.

He was weary of it.

She was his wife. No one would know if they slept together—in fact everyone would be surprised that they hadn't already. And he'd given her a taste of his own passion back there in the orchard and she hadn't pulled away. He'd told her that he wasn't the man for a sheltered virgin and she hadn't cared.

What was he trying to prove anyway? And who was he trying to prove it to?

Yes, he was supposed to be setting an example, to be better than Renzo Accorsi, but what went on in his bedroom had nothing to do with his country, and both his father and his mother were gone.

It was only sex. Sleeping with his wife wouldn't destroy his throne.

Anyway, she'd made the decision to put herself in his way, naked and on her knees. She wanted him and had made no secret of it. So now she'd have to accept the consequences.

He kicked the door shut behind him and walked over to the bed. It was gratifying to see how her gaze roved over his naked form, as if she liked what she saw as much as he did when he looked at her.

'You want me to be your husband, then?' he asked, pinning her with his gaze. 'In every way?'

She nodded, the pulse at the base of her pale throat beating frantically. 'Yes.'

He let himself look at her finally. Taking his time as he scanned every inch of her lovely body. She was so very, very pretty.

She is yours. Claim her.

Perhaps he would. Perhaps he'd claim her completely, permanently. He needed a wife anyway, to provide heirs, and any children they had would be the ultimate union of Benedictus and Accorsi. So why not this woman he already knew he wanted?

Of course they might not suit sexually, but he didn't think that would be the case. Even now he knew that one night wouldn't be enough for him, and a king couldn't be seen to be taking new lovers every couple of weeks. No, it was better to have one woman, and to have that woman be his wife.

'If you want this,' he said—because these would be his terms and she had to agree to them—'then understand that if we sleep together I will not give you a divorce later. You will remain my queen and carry my heirs.'

Her eyes widened. 'Oh, I—'

'I will not have a parade of lovers going in and out of my bedroom. That won't set the example I want for my rule or for my people. Also…' He paused so she would see his intention clearly in his face, so there would be no mistake. 'Now I have the throne, I will not give it up. The same goes for my queen. I keep what is mine, Guinevere Accorsi. So if you want me to be a husband to you, that is what you'll have to accept.'

She stared at him for a long moment and he watched in fascination as goosebumps rose on her skin. He wanted to touch her, stroke her, lick her all over like an ice cream. It felt almost impossible to hold himself back. But he wasn't going to touch her unless she accepted this. Because he had the feeling that if he did he wouldn't be able to give her up.

Slowly Guinevere nodded, and he could see fire in her blue gaze now, building higher and hotter. Little lioness. She was brave—he'd already seen evidence of that—but now he knew it to be true. Brave and passionate.

'I accept it,' she said in a husky voice. 'But I want something in return. For the duration of our marriage there will be no other women for you but me.'

As if he would want another woman. Looking at her, he couldn't even remember what other women looked like, and it satisfied him that she was asking for fidelity. He didn't want a doormat for a wife. He wanted a woman who demanded the same things of him that he did of her. A match for him. A meeting of equals. A queen had to be as strong as a king.

'I accept,' he said. 'There will no other women but you.'

She nodded, then slowly held out her arms to him. 'Then come to me, my king.'

My king...

The blood pumped hard in his veins at the husk in her voice, and at the way she held her arms out to him, welcoming him.

He came to the edge of the bed, looking down at her, kneeling before him, naked except for the veil of her hair.

His wife.

Lifting a hand, he threaded his fingers through her curls. Soft, like silk against his skin. 'You are mine,' he murmured. 'You are my war prize, little Accorsi, and so you must do whatever I tell you.'

She was trembling now, but it wasn't with fear—he could see that. No, there was nothing but hungry anticipation in her wide blue eyes.

'I will,' she whispered. 'What do want you me to do?'

He tightened his grip in her hair and then bent, answering her by taking her mouth in a hot, deep kiss. She tasted of oranges and sunshine and something else sweet, a flavour that he found the more he tasted, the more he wanted.

He kissed her deeper, hotter, and she made a small sound of hunger in the back of her throat that went straight to his groin. Before he knew what he was doing, he'd pushed her onto her back across the mattress and he was over her, tracking hot kisses down her neck and the delicate architecture of her throat, his hands tracing her curves as he went.

He lingered over her breasts, stroking, squeezing,

weighing them in his hands, before tracing the shape of them with his tongue, flicking over one hard little nipple before drawing it into his mouth. She cried out, her body arching against his, making him grit his teeth against the need to sink inside her straight away. He didn't want to do that yet. She was a virgin, and she was sheltered, and she'd been ill-treated. And despite all of that she'd chosen him to give herself to. And even though he'd told her he liked it rough, she deserved better from him than that. Certainly this first time. And besides, it was the perfect opportunity to drive her as mad as she'd driven him all day.

He licked and kissed and nipped her sensitive nipples, then worked his way down further, gripping her shuddering hips in his hands as he kissed his way over her stomach and finally down between her thighs.

Guinevere gave another hoarse cry as he tasted her, sweet yet tart at the same time, holding her writhing body as he explored. She panted and moaned, her hands in his hair, holding on to him as if she was drowning and he was the only thing keeping her afloat. He kept her there, exploring her deeper, drawing more and more desperate sounds from her as she moved restlessly beneath him, the grip she had in his hair almost painful.

She was as soft as he'd thought she'd be, and as hot, and she tasted like the sweetest treat. It felt as if he'd been years without a woman, years since he'd had anyone this responsive, this passionate. She'd abandoned herself to him without self-consciousness, not hiding her pleasure or holding back. It made him feel like a god that he could do this to her.

His little lioness.

She called his name in the end, as he brought her to the peak and held her there, making her plead, making her beg, and then he took her over it, her screams of release echoing in his ears.

Guinevere lay on her back in Tiberius's bed, staring blankly at the ceiling, trying to remember what her actual name was. It came back to her slowly as the aftershocks of that incredible climax faded, leaving her heavy and sated and yet strangely still hungry.

Guinevere. That was right. That was what her name was. And she was here in Tiberius's bed because she'd had the brilliant idea of giving herself to him in a way that would make it very difficult for him to refuse.

In fact, she'd gone through many scenarios after those moments in the orchard, trying to think of the best approach when it came to seducing her husband. But, considering how little experience she'd had with men, she'd decided that being as direct as possible was the key.

Of course he'd been working late, since that was what he'd been doing every night since he'd married her, so she'd had lots of time to prepare. Not that she'd needed it, since her plan had been basically to turn up naked in his bed.

She'd already been there a quite a while before he'd entered the bedroom, sitting on the bed, vacillating between wild excitement and a sick dread that he'd laugh at her, or simply send her away.

Anxiety had gripped her when she'd heard him enter the royal apartments, and then the shower in the bathroom next door had been turned on. Her heart beating fast, she'd come up onto her knees on the mattress, trying to calm her ragged nerves as she'd heard the door open.

Then he'd turned on the light and she'd seen him in the doorway.

Naked.

Her mouth had dried, her nerves forgotten, and she hadn't been able to look away. Because he was beautiful. So achingly beautiful. Broad shoulders. Muscled chest and stomach. Narrow hips and powerful thighs. All encased in smooth, satiny olive skin. And the most male part of him, hard and thick, making no secret of how much he wanted her.

She'd thrilled to it, even as a sudden attack of nerves had nearly undone her.

She'd thought he might turn around and walk away, leaving her kneeling in his bed all alone. She'd had no idea what she would do if that happened.

But it hadn't.

Instead, he'd told her that there would be no divorce. That if she wanted this then she had to accept that she would be his wife in every way, including bearing his heirs. She understood why. Knew that he wanted to set an example for his people. It wasn't about her specifically. It was about what she represented as his wife and queen.

She'd known a moment's hesitation when he'd laid it all out for her, because she hadn't been expecting that. Hadn't been expecting more than a night and hadn't thought about anything beyond that.

Yet he had.

She'd also known that this was the moment of truth. That if she didn't give this to him she'd get nothing at all. And looking at him, standing there, she hadn't been sure she could stand having nothing.

If she agreed, she would be his, and there was reassurance in being someone's...in being claimed. No one had ever wanted her to be theirs, even when she was a child, long before she'd decided that hiding was better than being noticed. Her value as a daughter, as her father had often said, was only in her ability to make a good marriage, nothing more.

Certainly no one had loved her, and while she knew that it wasn't love with Tiberius, she would settle for being desired. He'd promised to protect her too, and after all it would hardly be a hardship to share his bed every night.

Of course she'd said yes.

And then everything had happened very fast.

His lips on hers, his hands on her body, and then she'd been pushed onto her back and his marauding mouth had been everywhere. On her throat, her nipples, her thighs and then between.

Pleasure had gripped her like music as he'd turned her body into an instrument that he played with the most incredible precision. She hadn't known that so many different sounds could be drawn from her.

He hadn't been rough like he'd warned her earlier that day. Instead he'd been decisive, firm and unhesitating, which had thrilled her...excited her. She'd loved him taking charge, because she wouldn't have even known where to start.

Now she lay there, gasping, and he was moving again, sliding between her thighs, one hand braced beside her head as the other slipped through her slick folds, spreading her open for him. She stared up into his silver eyes as he shifted once again, pushing against her and then into her, sliding in deeply, slowly, watching her as he did so, gauging her reaction.

'Does this hurt?' he asked, his voice almost guttural.

She was panting, the feeling of him inside her almost too much and yet also not enough. 'No… It's just… strange.'

His hand slipped beneath her rear, lifting her, letting him slide even deeper, and then he paused. The feel of his hot, bare skin against hers and the weight of him on her was intensely erotic. She wanted to hold him there, never let him go.

Unexpectedly, he put out a hand and pushed a curl behind her ear, the movement tender, making her frantically beating heart catch fire. And then he leaned down and kissed her, tasting her, and at the same time he began to move, making her blaze.

She'd had no idea she could be so hungry for him again, and so soon, but she was. Desperate and feverish. Wanting more.

Looking up into his face, at the harshly carved lines of it drawn taut with desire, she felt the flames inside her burn higher and hotter. It was strange to be so surrounded by a person. To have him over her and inside her, the heat of his body against hers, the scent of his skin everywhere.

It was thrilling. Intoxicating.

She didn't know what to do with her hands, so she put them on his powerful shoulders, loving the feeling of hard muscle moving under his skin. The hand beneath her rear shifted again, tilting her hips, and somehow the hunger deepened, becoming fierce. Then it slid away as he reached down to grip her behind her knee, drawing her leg up and around his hip, opening her more to him.

'Better?' he asked roughly.

'Yes…' It came out on a gasp, the acuteness of the pleasure making her moan. 'Yes… More.'

Tiberius bent and kissed her, then his mouth moved down to her throat, the sharp edges of his teeth grazing the delicate cords of her neck. 'You enjoy this?' he growled, and the deep velvet sound of it was like a stroke against her skin. 'Giving yourself to a Benedictus? To your father's enemy?'

Maybe it was wrong to find that so erotic, but she did. 'Yes,' she moaned again. 'I like it. I want more.'

He moved faster, harder, and she began to understand what he meant by roughness, because he wasn't gentle. His grip was almost painful. But she loved it. It made her feel strong that he didn't hold himself back. It made her feel powerful.

'More,' she repeated, turning it into a demand. 'Don't hold back from me, my king. I'm not as delicate as you think.'

He growled then, and before she could take another breath he pulled out of her, flipping her over onto her front. Then he gripped her hips hard and slid back inside her from behind, moving faster, harder, deeper.

Guinevere pressed her hot face into the pillow as pleasure drew into a tight knot inside her, the pressure almost unbearable. Then he slipped a finger beneath her, finding the most sensitive part of her, stroking firmly. And that hard, tight knot burst suddenly apart.

She screamed against the pillow as the orgasm crashed over her, and as she shook and shook she dimly felt him move faster, then fall out of rhythm, heard his own harsh roar of release in her ears.

She lay there for several stunned seconds, listened to both of them breathing hard. Then with firm hands he withdrew from her, before pulling her into the warmth of his body, turning her over onto her back and taking her chin between his fingers. His burning gaze swept over her, as if checking she was unharmed, before settling on her face.

'Did I hurt you?' he asked. 'Give me the truth, now, lioness.'

'No,' she said huskily, tremors still shaking her. 'Not at all.'

He said nothing for a long moment, and she was distracted by the dark shadows beneath his eyes, the lines around his mouth. He had been working hard. Perhaps too hard.

Without thinking, she reached up and touched his cheek. 'You look tired.'

'I am.' He made no move to avoid her touch, only stared down at her as if he couldn't look away. 'But I couldn't go to sleep because someone was already in my bed.'

The faint trace of humour in his voice was unexpected, and she smiled. 'Sorry. I thought the direct approach was better.'

'I'm not complaining.' He turned his head against her hand, brushing her fingertips with his mouth. 'You're very brave, though. To beard me in my den, so to speak. Especially after what I told you today.'

'I think your bark is worse than your bite.'

His eyes glinted wickedly. 'How can you know when I haven't bitten you yet?'

A delicious shiver ran through her. 'When you said that you like it rough...is biting a part of that?'

'Sometimes.' He leaned down and kissed her again. 'I meant what I said,' he murmured against her mouth. 'You will be in my bed every night, and you will be my wife in every way from now on. Do you understand?'

She sighed, the feel of his mouth on hers like a cold drink of water in a parched desert. 'Yes.'

He trailed kisses down her throat. 'And I will not divorce you. You will stay my queen from now on.'

Another sigh escaped her as, unbelievably, her body began to wake once more. 'Yes,' she repeated.

He lifted his mouth from hers, then took her hand, guiding it to the hard, flat plane of his stomach and down. His skin was hot, and it felt like satin, and she was once more hungry.

'Shall I show you the proper respect that a war prize should give to her king?'

Her mouth went dry as he wrapped her fingers around the rapidly hardening length of his shaft. 'P-please...'

So he showed her how to touch him, how to caress him—and, no, she didn't have to be gentle. She could be rough as she wanted. Then he guided her mouth to him, so she could worship him there, as he'd worshipped her, and she loved it.

He tasted good, and the feel of him in her mouth was good too, and when that got too much he pulled her up and lifted her, settling her down on him and showing her how to ride him.

In fact, he showed her many other things too, keeping her up well into the night. And she didn't even think about going to her little room, not once. Instead she fell asleep in his arms, exhausted.

CHAPTER SEVEN

THE LIMO DROVE slowly through the streets of Kasimir's capital city, with Tiberius gazing out through the windows at the crowds thronging the footpaths. They were cheering and waving Kasimiran flags, children were being lifted up by their parents to catch a glimpse of the King's car.

It was gratifying to find the people so excited to see him. Certainly his aides had mentioned that the mood of the country was high—far better than it had been when the Accorsis were in power, which pleased him.

Of course there was still much work to be done, but this public appearance—a tour of the city's main hospital—would be the start of many, and would hopefully provide the people with much-needed reassurance.

Guinevere sat beside him. She was in a yellow dress today, gauzy and pretty, wrapping around her curves lovingly, while her hair was piled on top of her head, with a couple of loose curls trailing around her ears.

She looked delicate and beautiful, like a splash of sunshine sitting beside him, and already anticipation was gathering tight inside him at the thought of showing this lovely, lovely woman to his subjects and introducing her as his new queen.

There would no doubt be some trepidation about the fact that she was an Accorsi, and he'd already anticipated that, but they would soon come to see that she was nothing like her father.

He knew that now for the truth, having spent the past week with her.

It had been a revelation.

He'd still been working every hour, closeted with his advisors and talking over things like taxes and elections, but every night he'd found himself hurrying back to the royal apartments and to Guinevere.

She slept in his bed every night, in his arms, languorous and sated as a cat after hours of extremely satisfying sex. She was passionate and curious, responsive and generous, and he'd never had a lover like her. It seemed the more he had of her, the more he wanted, and he certainly had no regrets about his decision to keep her as his wife.

Not that they'd spoken about the future of their marriage. He simply hadn't had the time. And in the hours he did spend with her he preferred to pursue their physical hunger for each other over anything else.

She hadn't argued, seemingly as hungry for him as he was for her.

A couple of days earlier she'd asked him if he'd have some time to talk about her role as queen, but he hadn't yet followed that up. There always seemed to be more important, more vital things to do.

He glanced at her now, assessing her. She was looking out of the window too, her cheeks a little pale, her hands clasped tightly in her lap, lines of tension around her eyes.

Reaching out, he took one of her hands in his. Her fingertips were cold. 'Nervous?' he asked softly.

She glanced away from the window and back at him. 'Yes, a little.'

'What about?'

'Oh…the crowds. I haven't ever been among so many people at one time. And also…' She let out a breath. 'I'm an Accorsi.'

The protective urge he felt whenever he was around her stirred again, and he squeezed her hand gently in reassurance. 'I will allow no one to hurt you, remember?' He put the force of all his considerable authority behind the words. 'And I will allow no one to show you any disrespect. You are my queen and I expect everyone to treat you accordingly.'

She looked down at where her hand was enclosed by his. 'I don't feel like your queen,' she said. 'I feel like your dirty little secret.'

The comment came out of the blue, and for a moment he could only stare at her in surprise. 'What? What makes you say that?'

She didn't reply immediately, still staring at her hands. Then she sighed. 'Sorry, I didn't mean it to come out sounding that way. It's just… You're not around during the day, and I only see you at night, only in bed. And we don't talk. We just have sex.'

He frowned. 'Is that a problem?'

'Yes. I would like to talk to you, Tiberius. I want to

know what kind of marriage we're going to have—especially since you were so demanding about it before we slept together. And I want to know what kind of role I'll have in the palace, because at the moment I don't have one.'

He was conscious then of a slight shock—because these were things he hadn't considered. He'd been so consumed with getting his country in order that he hadn't had the time to consider anything personal.

'I sent an aide to you yesterday,' he pointed out—because he had. 'To prepare you for today's appearance.'

'Yes, you did,' she allowed. 'But…'

Annoyance was starting to creep through him—mostly at himself for not sparing a moment to think about her. 'But what?' he asked, trying not to let his irritation show. 'I have had a great deal to manage, Guinevere. Naturally I apologise if I've neglected you, but the wellbeing of my country takes precedence.'

She looked at him for a long moment, then abruptly pulled her hand from his. 'I'm not asking you to ignore the wellbeing of Kasimir. In fact, I want to be a part of helping you rebuild it. But I don't know how to be a queen and I don't know what's required. I don't know what your plans for the future are, or what my place is in that future.' Her chin came up. 'It feels as if you're ashamed of me.'

Tiberius was conscious of not a little astonishment. 'Ashamed of you?' he repeated. 'Why would I be ashamed of you?'

'Because I'm an Accorsi,' Guinevere said. 'Because

I'm sheltered and I don't know anything. Because I'm not—'

Tiberius laid a gentle finger over her soft mouth, silencing her. 'I'm not ashamed of you,' he said. 'I married you *because* you were an Accorsi. Because I wanted Kasimir to be whole, not divided.'

That hot blue flame of her temper had begun to burn in her eyes and she reached up, gripped his wrist and pulled his finger away. 'I don't want to be a symbol, Tiberius. I want to do something. I've spent years being trapped in that damn palace, and if I'm to be your queen I need to know how. I already know what it's like to be forgotten and I'm tired of it.'

Then, as if to emphasise her point, she nipped the end of his finger, sending a bolt of white heat through him and making his breath catch.

'If you do not wish to give our people a ringside seat for what I do to you at night,' he growled, 'I would advise against doing things like that.'

She dropped his hand, but gave him an unrepentant look. 'If you want your war prize ready, willing and eager every night, then I would advise giving me something to do.'

Stubborn little Accorsi!

She's not wrong.

Looked at from her point of view, that was of course how she would see it. And, no, she wasn't wrong. He hadn't given her any time this past week, nor spared her a thought beyond what they did in bed together. Of course there were things they needed to discuss, he just...

You just don't want to think about her. You don't want to think about another person's needs.

And how could he when the needs of his subjects mattered more? Then again, if she was to be his queen, then not teaching her what she needed to know was shortsighted. Especially if she could help him in his endeavours. He wasn't used to sharing the burden, it was true, but that wasn't because he didn't want to share it with someone.

He met her gaze and held it. 'I see your point. For the record, I am genuinely *not* ashamed of you, little lioness. I have just been very busy with trying to fix everything that is broken in Kasimir—and there is so much that is broken.'

The sparks of her temper faded, her blue gaze turning softer. 'I know,' she said quietly. 'I do know that. But the state Kasimir is in is not your fault, Tiberius. You understand that, don't you?'

Another little shock went through him, as if she'd somehow found a vulnerable place inside him. 'I know that,' he said tersely, sounding far more defensive than he wished. 'Of course it isn't my fault. Why would you think I believe that?'

She ignored his tone. 'Because of the way you're trying to fix it. As if you alone are responsible for it.'

'But isn't it my responsibility? I am the King. It is my job to protect and care for my subjects.' And before he could stop himself, he added, 'If it hadn't taken me so long to reclaim the crown, there wouldn't have been—'

'No,' Guinevere interrupted, gently but very firmly. 'You can't think that. My father stole the crown and he is to blame for what happened—not you. Also, you can't take the burden of repairing an entire country upon yourself. That's ridiculous. Besides, how can you take care of anyone else if you don't take care of yourself?'

'I don't need taking care of,' he said, again far too tersely.

'Of course you do,' she disagreed. 'You're working yourself to the bone and everyone else around you too. The burden can be shared, you know.'

It was as if she'd reached inside his head and plucked out that very thought.

Of course it could be shared. Except no one had ever offered to do so because they were worried about *him*... as if *his* wellbeing mattered to them. His father had made sure he was fed and clothed, and had taught him all he needed to know about being a king. But his father hadn't been concerned for Tiberius himself. All that had been important was being strong enough to take the crown and then to take responsibility for the country. His own wellbeing had always come last.

'I do not matter,' he said. 'Only Kasimir does.'

Guinevere's deep blue eyes were soft. 'You do matter,' she said quietly. 'You matter to me.'

That softness, the way she was looking at him, rubbed against a raw place inside him—a place he hadn't thought was vulnerable. 'Why should you care?' he demanded, unable to keep the edge out of his voice. 'You barely know me.'.

'Why should I care?' she repeated, her eyes widening in surprise. 'Because I'm your wife and your queen and because someone has to, Tiberius. You can't do this all on your own.'

He wasn't sure why he wanted to argue with her—tell her that he'd been doing this all on his own since his father had died and he'd succeeded very well, thank you very much. He wasn't sure, either, why there was a curious leaden feeling in his gut…as if he'd wanted her to say something else, though what, he didn't know.

Right then, though, the limo came to a stop outside the hospital and it was time for them to get out.

'I am not doing this on my own,' he said curtly. 'Now it's your turn to help.'

Guinevere's mouth had gone dry and her stomach was unsettled with nerves. The conversation with Tiberius had distracted her from the upcoming appearance, but unfortunately it hadn't made her feel any more settled.

She'd spent the past week roaming around the palace, familiarising herself with going outside, as well as looking up on a computer all the articles about the state of Kasimir she could find, and then looking in vain for aides who could give her information about what she was supposed to be doing.

She'd hoped Tiberius would give her some time so she could discuss with him her thoughts, but he'd been incommunicado for most of the week. Busy, his aides would tell her. His Majesty had no time to spare.

Except for the nights, of course, when he had plenty of time to spare, and when all discussions fell by the wayside in favour of the physical pleasure they could give one another. She had only herself to blame for that, she supposed, but he made her feel so good, and it was easier in the end to let her body do the talking.

As the week had gone on she'd started to feel more and more annoyed with both herself and him, but it wasn't until now, when she had him for a length of time out of the bedroom, that she'd thought she might as well take advantage of that.

She hadn't meant to sound so cross, but that had been her nerves talking. But then, when he'd told her about his responsibilities, all her annoyance at him had just leaked away.

Because all it had taken was one look into his fierce silver gaze to see that he believed utterly that, being the King, it was his responsibility to repair the country and his alone. That he cared about it and cared very deeply. That he worried for his subjects. That the length of time it had taken for him to get rid of the tyrants ate at him. And whether he knew it or not, some part of him must blame himself for that. Otherwise why would he be so impatient to fix everything?

It made her feel petty for being angry with him at not giving her any time—but, petty or not, the fact remained that there were things they needed to discuss.

Also, she wanted to help. Kasimir was her country too, and if she was going to be its queen she wanted to be a practical one, not a mere figurehead. Her father had nearly run the country into the ground, therefore it was her responsibility to fix it as well as Tiberius's.

Being with him, telling him what she wanted, had given her courage, and she didn't want to go back to hiding safely in the walls of the palace any more—even though she might be nervous about what the people would think of her.

Those nerves were certainly making themselves felt now, as the limo door opened, letting in the noise and the cheering of the crowd.

Tiberius got out first, the cheers rising in volume as he appeared, and no wonder.

He wore a dark suit today, with a plain white shirt and a silvery grey silk tie that set his eyes off to perfection. He was astonishingly charismatic, and she couldn't help but watch him, mesmerised, as he acknowledged the crowds, a smile turning his beautiful mouth.

She shivered, unable to help herself, still tasting the salt from his skin where she'd nipped him. She shouldn't have done it, but she hadn't been able to resist, because he was irresistible. Even when she was arguing with him she wanted to touch him, kiss him. Wanted to be close to him.

He turned back to the limo and his dark head bent as he leaned down to offer her his hand. And then she was being drawn out of the car to stand beside him, the roar of the crowd in her ears.

It was almost overwhelming, the number of people and the noise, and she didn't know quite where to look—especially when she heard a couple of boos in amongst all the cheering. A few people were even carrying signs that had derogatory statements about her family on them.

She couldn't blame those people, but it made her feel

anxious. Not so much that they would hurt her, but that her presence at Tiberius's side would damage his political standing as King. Yes, marrying her would show his willingness to move on as a whole country rather than as one divided, and that was a good thing, but there would always be those who would view that as a betrayal.

Abruptly, the thought of her presence undermining his rule made her feel afraid. Although he hadn't told her anything about his life in exile, she had got the impression that it had been a hard and long journey back to his crown, and certainly the time and effort he'd put into his first week as King could not be understated.

She hoped her presence wouldn't put all that work at risk.

Why would you care?

Good question. But it was one she knew the answer to, and one she'd given to him already. He mattered to her. And whether that was because of the sex or something else, she didn't know. But matter to her he did.

His hand was warm around hers, and he didn't let it go as she came to stand beside him. So when he moved over to where some of the crowds were standing behind the barriers she had no choice but to follow him.

Had he heard the people booing her? Had he seen those signs?

'Don't be afraid,' he murmured in her ear, showing her that, yes, indeed, he had seen the signs. 'They are only a small proportion of this crowd and they do not know you.'

'I don't want to undermine you,' she whispered back. 'And I'm afraid my presence here will.'

He paused for a moment, in full view of the crowd, though she was pretty sure no one could actually hear them.

'Your presence undermines nothing.' His gaze was fierce. 'You are strong and beautiful and brave—everything our people require in a queen. So show them, my little lioness. Show them what kind of queen they are getting.'

He had taken to calling her that whenever she lay in his arms, and she liked it a lot. She liked the conviction in his eyes too. He wasn't a man for idle words, and he meant what he said when he said it.

The way he looked at her made her feel as if she was every one of those things, and the nerves in her stomach settled. And so, obeying an impulse she hadn't seen coming, she went on her toes and kissed him in front of the crowd.

The cheers were almost deafening as she came back down on her feet, and when she looked up into his face and saw the look of shock there she smiled at him. Then, gripping hard to her courage, she approached the crowd, smiling at them too, speaking a few words to some of the people.

A little girl pushed some flowers into her hands and said breathlessly, 'You're so pretty!' And another young woman wanted a selfie.

Tiberius joined her, and together they moved towards the hospital entrance, pausing to speak to as many people as they could.

By the time they got through the hospital doors

Guinevere was breathless. Her face hurt from smiling, and she felt energised in a way she'd never felt before.

It might only have been a small proportion of the population here today, but there had been more who'd welcomed her than who hadn't, and it had been wonderful.

For so long she'd felt powerless and alone, but here, at Tiberius's side, she didn't feel like his dirty little secret now. She felt like his queen.

This is how you can make a difference. This is how you can right the wrongs done to you and your country. This is how you can defeat the ghosts of your father and your brothers.

Determination settled inside her as they were introduced to the hospital management. She was an Accorsi, and while what had happened to her country hadn't been her fault, or Tiberius's, it was something she wanted to fix, nevertheless. It was right that an Accorsi should help to put right all the wrongs. It was how it should be. And she wasn't going to be put off by Tiberius any longer.

Tonight she wasn't going to let him sequester himself away with his aides. She was going to demand they discuss all things to do with their marriage, and then she was going to join him in his meetings.

And she was not going to take no for an answer.

The hospital visit was appalling in some ways, because it made clear the depth of underfunding for critical health services. But it was good for both her and Tiberius to know, because once they did they could do all they could to fix it.

The visit took up most of the day, and by the time

they got back to the palace it was close to evening. As they got out of the limo, Tiberius said, 'I have a meeting to attend. I don't know what time—'

'No,' she interrupted, looking at him stubbornly. 'That can wait. The meeting you have to attend is one with me.'

He frowned. 'It is to discuss taxation. That will end up funding the hospital we just saw, which desperately needs the money.'

Guinevere let out a breath. 'There will always be something more important, Tiberius. The taxation discussion can wait for at least one hour, can't it?'

He regarded her silently for a moment. 'Very well,' he said at last. 'I can spare you an hour.'

They retired to his office, with Tiberius pausing outside the door to ask for some food to be brought to them, since they hadn't eaten since the lunch the hospital had put on.

Then he gestured for Guinevere to come in, before shutting the door firmly behind them.

'Very well,' he said, coming to stand in front of the fireplace, his muscular arms folded. 'You want a discussion…so let us discuss.'

He looked forbidding standing there, and very stern. The smile she'd seen him give to so many people today was absent now. He didn't want to be here, she could tell, and she could almost sense the tightly leashed impatient energy crackling around his tall figure.

He still looked tired, and unexpectedly her heart ached. He was so driven. It couldn't be easy to think that you were ultimately responsible for an entire country, and to be so conscious of it with every passing second. He could afford some time here and there just for himself, couldn't he?

Then another thought struck her. If he didn't look after himself, who was there to do it for him? Who did he have to turn to when things were hard? Who did he talk to honestly and openly? Did he have anyone he trusted? Anyone at all?

You know he doesn't.

Oh, she knew that. She knew all too well. Just as she knew what it was like to be lonely. To have no one. She'd had no one for so very long and it had been so very difficult.

Perhaps if he truly had no one she could be that person for him?

All of a sudden she wanted to be. She very much wanted to be.

'When was the last time you had a break?' she asked.

His black brows drew down. 'A break? What do you mean by "a break"?'

'A holiday, Tiberius. Time off to relax.'

'A holiday?' he echoed, repeating the words as if they were in a foreign language. 'You think that I have time for...holidays?'

'I think you tell yourself you don't have time for them. But be honest. How long have you been working for Kasimir without a break?'

CHAPTER EIGHT

T<small>IBERIUS STOOD IN FRONT</small> of the fireplace, his arms folded across his chest, staring at his wife, who was staring back as she stood in a patch of late-afternoon sunlight looking as if she glowed from within.

She'd been remarkable today. Yes, she'd been nervous, but when she'd stepped out of the limo and had joined him on a walkabout with the crowd she'd been... amazing. Warm and open and approachable, radiating her beautiful smile.

He'd seen the signs of a few dissenters within the crowd, had heard them booing her. As he'd told her, they were only a small percentage, and even though he'd burned to do something incredibly inappropriate, such as punching them in the face, he'd controlled himself and ignored them instead.

He'd appreciated her sharing her worries with him, about how her presence might undermine what he was trying to do, but she needn't be concerned.

While she might be an Accorsi, she was one who wasn't known to the world's press, and thus there was no gossip about her. No rumours. No hidden videos or toxicity that might rear its ugly head online at the worst possible time.

There was only her, beautiful in her yellow dress, her smile like the promise of summer on a cold winter day. She was honest and open, not a shred of darkness in her.

As his queen, she was perfect.

Really, he shouldn't begrudge her this time she wanted for a discussion, since if she wanted to take an active part in ruling they would need to talk about it. But this mention of holidays…

What on earth was she talking about? Who could think of breaks or holidays when they had a country to run? A country where people had suffered and were suffering still?

A holiday implied personal whim, and Giancarlo had been very clear that kings did not indulge in personal whims. There was no rest for a king. Responsibility was a heavy weight that had to be endured.

'I have been working for Kasimir since the day I was born,' he said severely. 'My mother died in the coup— you know this, yes?'

She nodded slowly. 'I do know. I'm sorry that—'

'It's not your fault. She died before you were born. Renzo's guards shot her as she was escaping with my father, and to save me he had to leave her behind.'

Her eyes darkened. 'That's awful.'

'Your father didn't offer her any medical help so she bled to death.' He hadn't meant for the words to sound so stark, especially when an expression that looked like pain crossed her features. But he didn't take them back.

That was what had happened—no more and certainly no less.

'That must have been dreadful,' she said softly.

He shrugged, ignoring the pain that sat inside him. 'I don't remember her, but certainly doing the best for Kasimir that I can is how I will make her and my father's sacrifice worth it.'

She nodded slowly. 'And then you went into exile with your father?'

'Yes, we escaped into Italy. But I did not have a normal childhood. My responsibilities were made clear to me before I'd even started school.'

Her brow creased. 'Did no one help you? Did no one…?'

'What? Interfere politically with a tiny European nation? No, no one helped. And, no, my father didn't take me on holiday anywhere. He was of the opinion that a king has no personal life. He is a servant of his people and they come before him every time.'

Her gaze flickered briefly at that, but all she said was, 'So…what? You've been training to be a king all this time?'

'Of course. Did you think I just strolled into the palace the day we met? No, my father and I had to find supporters, work to raise funds, and then get sympathisers from within Kasimir itself, because we didn't want a civil war.'

'So…you never had a chance just to be a boy?'

There was something soft in her eyes that felt dangerous, though he wasn't sure why.

'No. People were dying here. People were suffering. There was no time "just to be a boy".'

She took a small step towards him. 'When will it end, Tiberius? This concern? This frantic need to fix everything?'

What strange questions she was asking him. Questions she should know the answers to if she thought long enough about them.

'It won't ever end,' he said. 'People will always suffer and something will always be broken. The responsibility of a king is a burden without end.'

That soft expression on her face deepened, and it looked like concern. 'But,' she murmured, 'is there any time in all of that for yourself? For joy? For happiness?'

Joy. Happiness.

He couldn't remember ever feeling either of those emotions. Maybe once, when he was a child, lying on his back looking at the stars, he'd felt something akin to them. But it had been so long ago now he couldn't remember what they felt like. And anyway, he'd managed well enough without them so far. Why would he need them now? Why should he have them when some of his subjects could not?

He'd always been cognisant of the fact that his life was not his own and never had been. He was the son of a dispossessed king. His mother had given up her own life for him. And then his father had died of cancer, five years ago, and now he had to make those deaths meaningful. He had been saved for a reason, his father had told him from his hospital bed, just before he'd died.

And that reason was to restore the crown, help the people of Kasimir.

'No,' he said impatiently. 'Why should I have either of those when many of my subjects do not? I have power, Guinevere, and I do not take that lightly. Nor can I rest on it. The work is always there and must always be done—so, no, there can be no rest from it.'

She swallowed, a flicker of what looked like anguish crossing her features. 'Is that what our marriage will be, then?' she asked quietly. 'You working until midnight every night and then rising at dawn the next day? Where is there time for children in that? Where is there time for a marriage? A life?'

Something caught at his heart then, giving a small, painful tug. 'There will be time for children,' he said, ignoring it. 'I will have a schedule and they'll be looked after. We will engage the services of a nanny, naturally.'

'But what about time as a family?' She was searching his face as if looking for something. 'Surely there will be time for that?'

'Not at the expense of the work I must do for Kasimir.' He was getting impatient now, because these conversations weren't important right now—couldn't she see that? They could be had later. 'Our family will not look like those of other people because we are a royal family,' he added. 'As I said, our purpose is to serve our country, not vice versa.'

'So, what you're saying is that there is no time for any kind of personal happiness?' she said, an edge in her voice now. 'No time for joy?'

'You may have joy and happiness.' He was holding on

to his patience by a thread. 'I am not saying you can't have that. But you need to understand that the lives of rulers are hard ones, contrary to what most people think. It is our cross to bear and our privilege.'

A strange expression crossed her face, one that he couldn't interpret. 'That seems very bleak.'

'Struggle is the anvil we temper ourselves upon,' he said, quoting his father's favourite line. 'And my father gave me plenty of struggle to help prepare me for my role.'

'He didn't...?' She stopped, pain in her voice.

Tiberius knew what she was asking, though. 'No,' he said, this time softening his tone. 'He was never cruel. But he expected a lot from me, and I admit there were times when it was...difficult.' He paused a moment, wanting to give her something that wasn't as bleak, because he was sure it actually hadn't been as terrible as all that. 'Sometimes, as a child, I had difficulty sleeping, so I'd get up and go outside, lie down in the grass to watch the stars. It was...peaceful.'

'That's the only good thing you remember?'

He stared back at her. 'Why does it matter that there were good things? My father did what he had to—which was to put his country first by training me, so my mother's death wouldn't be for nothing.'

She held his gaze a moment, then looked away. 'It just sounds hard,' she said after a moment.

'It was hard,' he agreed. 'But life is not meant to be easy. You yourself know this already, Guinevere. It isn't as if you had an ideal childhood either.'

He wasn't sure why she seemed to find his past quite so painful, especially in comparison to the prison of hers.

'No, I didn't.' She glanced down at the floor. 'My brothers were not…kind.'

Tiberius frowned at the catch in her voice. He hadn't wanted to press her about exactly what her brothers had done to her, but now he couldn't stop himself from asking, 'What did they do, lioness?'

She looked wordlessly at him then, blue eyes dark.

'You don't have to tell me,' he went on. 'Not if you don't want to.'

And he meant it. He found he didn't want to cause her any unnecessary pain.

She stayed silent for a long time, and he thought that maybe she wouldn't, but then she said, 'It…doesn't sound bad…not compared to what some people have to suffer, but… They terrified me and I think they… liked that. They used to h-hunt me in the hallways— that's what they called it, Hunt the Mouse—just to scare me. And they pulled my hair, broke my toys, pushed me into walls, and once Alessio gave me a black eye.'

Tiberius was almost stupefied by a hot rush of fury so intense he could hardly keep still. He'd not heard any rumours about Renzo's sons, but this wasn't a rumour. This was the truth, he could hear the ring of it in her voice.

They'd *hunted* her. *Terrified* her. And all for fun, by the sounds of it.

He'd never wanted to hurt anyone as badly as he wanted to hurt her brothers.

'And your father?' he forced out, his voice hoarse with fury. 'What did he do about it?'

She shook her head. 'Nothing. He indulged them... told me that's what brothers did.'

'Guinevere,' he said roughly, taking a step towards her to take her hand, offer her something—he didn't know what.

But then she lifted her head and looked at him, her blue eyes clear. 'I hid from them in the end, because that was safer, and then they forgot about me. It wasn't all bad, though—and I mean that. I had moments of happiness. Reading good books in my little room. Listening to music. Watching movies. Learning about the outside world. I just loved that.'

He could see her as little girl. Long golden curls and wide blue eyes alight with the same joy he'd seen when he'd showed her the orchard. Her ready laugh and her smile, despite what she'd been through.

She was made for joy, he thought suddenly. Standing there in her yellow dress, she was made for sunshine and summer and moments of happiness.

You cannot give her that. You will never give her that.

The thought came out of nowhere, startling him, pulling at something painful inside him. It was true. He couldn't give her that. He barely even recognised happiness, let alone would be able to give it to her.

Yet you have tied her to you for ever.

That painful thing tugged harder, and he almost growled at it. Yes, he *had* made the decision to keep her—and he didn't regret it. She was a strong woman. She would find her own happiness, her own joy. It didn't have to come from him. That was one of the down-sides of marrying a king: the work always had to come first. He'd given her a choice, anyway. She hadn't had to choose to stay married to him.

A part of him told him snidely that that was specious reasoning, but he didn't want to dig into it any further. It was what it was.

'Well,' he said, when she didn't say anything more, 'is there something else you wish to discuss?'

She stared at him a moment longer, then said, 'I want to take part in your meetings. If I am to be your queen, then I want to be more than just a symbol to the people. I want to actually do something.'

She had mentioned something similar in the limo that morning, and he'd found her desire to be involved admirable.

You will need to spend time with her, teaching her.

He didn't have the time to show her personally, but he could spare an aide to show her the ropes.

'Of course,' he said. 'I will have someone come to you tomorrow morning, if you like. They can spend some time with you and—'

'No,' Guinevere interrupted, for the second time that day. 'I don't want one of your aides. I want you to do it.'

By the set of Tiberius's mouth and the flash of temper in his silver eyes Guinevere knew that he didn't like that idea at all. But that was too bad. If that was the only way she could get her husband out of his meetings and spending time with her, then that was what she'd do.

The idea had come to her as they'd discussed his utter

disdain for holidays. Not that she'd expected anything else—especially given what he'd said about his father driving him and his mother's death. She felt sorry for that little boy whose only peace had been looking at the stars. Such a heavy burden to put on his shoulders.

It made her understand him a little bit better, though. Gave her some insight into why he was so driven, why everything was of such vital importance, and why he had to be the one to fix it.

He was inured to fighting now, to struggle—she could see it in his eyes just as clearly as she saw his weariness.

He didn't know what joy was, what happiness was, either. And for some reason that hurt. He was a prickly, driven man, who desperately needed some kind of surcease. More than what she gave him in bed, certainly.

Perhaps she shouldn't have told him about what her brothers had done to her, because that hadn't helped— she hadn't missed the hot leap of rage in his gaze in response. But he'd called her lioness, and that had made her brave, and while he might not have been aware of it, telling him the truth had been a gift of trust. And he'd reined in his protector's rage, not burdening her with it.

He didn't know what he'd given her—didn't know why being able to tell him and not suffer any judgment was important. She wasn't sure he'd want to hear it anyway. But she wanted to give him something in return. If not happiness, then peace. Rest. A moment of lightness amidst the hard grind of his work.

But she was going to have to teach him. She knew it deep inside. Because if she didn't, this was what the shape of her marriage would be. Seeing him at night only, with his country constantly taking and taking from him. It wasn't the kind of marriage that people had in the books she'd read, and it certainly wasn't the kind of marriage she wanted to bring her children up in.

Why do you want that with him, though?

Because she'd married him. No, he hadn't given her much of a choice in the beginning, but he'd given it to her the night they'd first slept together. She'd told herself then, in a haze of desire, that she was fine with that—and she was still fine with it. But she was starting to want more. More of him. A chance to dig beneath the surface of the King and find the passionate man who lost himself in her arms every night.

And there was more there—she could sense it. He was like a fire burning in a cosy room and she was only looking at it through the window. She wanted to get closer to that fire…see how hot it really burned.

And even if those concerns were for herself, there were also potential children to consider. She wanted to give them a better childhood than the one she'd had, and certainly better than what Tiberius's father had given him. Was that really too much to ask?

So, yes, she would have to teach him what joy and happiness looked like, and she'd likely have to do it by stealth. She'd have to make him give her some time every day, and if she couched it in terms of it being for Kasimir's aid then surely he couldn't say no.

'No,' said Tiberius shortly. 'I do not have the time.'

'I'm not asking for much. A couple of hours every

day. Perhaps in the morning, when we wake up, or at night before bed?'

'Like I said—'

'It has to be you, Tiberius,' she said insistently. 'You're so passionate about Kasimir and none of your aides could teach me about being a queen better than you could. We have to rule together, remember? So wouldn't it be best for you to show me how you do it, so I can match you?'

His gaze narrowed, clearly looking for reasons to disagree, but she knew he couldn't argue with her last statement. After all, there *was* no one more passionate about Kasimir than he was, and if there was one thing she knew about him, it was that he was a control freak.

Perhaps he just doesn't want to spend time with you.

The thought made a sharp sliver of glass slide under her skin, cutting her in a way she hadn't been expecting, but she ignored it. If he didn't, he didn't—but she was going to make him give her this despite that. This wasn't about her and her needs. It was about him.

'A couple of hours…' he murmured, still eyeing her narrowly. 'That's not nearly enough time to learn how to be a queen. It took me many years before I fully grasped what being King meant.'

'Yes, it might take time,' she allowed. 'But I'll learn more directly from you than anyone else. Also, I could get further instruction from your aides when you're busy.' She gave him a sunny smile. 'I'm a quick study. I've been reading all I can about Kasimir—all the things that my father didn't tell me—so I'm familiar with its difficulties.'

He said nothing, still looking at her as if he was debating.

Guinevere moved over to him and placed her hands on his broad chest, loving the feel of him beneath her palms. He really was the most eminently touchable man… 'If you like,' she murmured, 'we could do it bed in the mornings. Or, if you'd prefer, before we retire at night.' She looked up at him from beneath her lashes. 'There must be more I need to learn about how to show proper respect for my king.'

As she'd hoped, the silver flames she'd become addicted to ignited, burned suddenly and intensely in his eyes. She really was getting the hang of flirting with him.

'Perhaps,' he said, his voice hot and rough. 'Perhaps there are…certain things I can teach you.'

Guinevere rose up on her toes and pressed her mouth gently to his. A soft, butterfly kiss. 'I'm sure you can, Your Majesty,' she whispered. 'I can hardly wait.'

His hands settled on her hips, holding her close. 'How about I give you a few tips now? Here?'

A shiver ran through her. He was never physically demanding outside of the bedroom. He would be absent all day and only at night would her take her, often in a wild rush, as if his desire was a river he kept behind a dam and only at night would he open the floodgates.

It felt intoxicating to ignite his passion this way…to make him forget his never-ending workload with only a kiss.

'I thought you had more important things to do?' she said, teasing just a little. 'Taxation, I think you mentioned.'

He frowned, his gaze dipping to her mouth and back

up again. She could feel him hardening against her, and the hot press of his body made her feel dizzy, as if she'd had too much champagne far too quickly.

'That can wait for a few minutes.'

A few minutes…

At night, when finally the day was done and they came together in bed, it was a flash fire. But they never indulged in any lazy aftermath, any idle conversation. Never simply enjoyed being together. He would take what he wanted, give her what she wanted, and then, inevitably, he would fall asleep. Because he was exhausted.

It would be like that now, she knew. They would take their pleasure, and it would be quick, hurried and intense, and then he would leave for yet another meeting, likely not coming back to bed until much later that night.

You are giving him everything he wants and he is giving you nothing in return.

That wasn't quite true. He gave her as much pleasure as she could handle, and then some. He wasn't a selfish lover by any stretch of the imagination. But she was starting to realise she wanted more than mere physical release. She wanted his time too.

Her own body was starting to wake, her hunger for him building, but she forced it away. He'd always been demanding about his own needs, but now it was time to give him a taste of his own medicine.

Guinevere reached down to where his hands gripped her hips and gently but firmly removed them. Then she forced herself to step back, her heart beating uncomfortably fast. 'No,' she said. 'I want more than just a few minutes.'

She had never denied him before, and it was gratifying to see his temper flare, a bright burst of silver. It made her aware of her own power to affect him, and that was satisfying too.

'What do you mean, more than a few minutes?' His voice was calm, but a muscle jumped in the side of his strong jaw.

'I mean exactly that.' She stepped back again. 'I don't want a few hurried minutes of pleasure.'

The muscle at the side of his jaw leapt again, the lines of his face growing tight with annoyance. 'We will have tonight also.'

'You mean with you falling asleep because you're exhausted?' She shook her head. 'I want more than that, Tiberius, and I think you owe it to me. I've given you everything you asked for. I haven't denied you a thing. So don't you think it's time for me to ask something of you?'

'I've just agreed to give you a couple of hours—'

'To teach me about being a queen, yes. I'm talking about us being together as husband and wife. Not me being the mistress you come to every night and leave before she wakes up every morning.'

He did not like that, it was clear. His whole body was tense. His hands had dropped to his sides and were clenched into fists. A week ago the signs of his anger would have terrified her, but since then she'd discovered the steel inside her—and besides, she knew he'd never hurt her.

'Guinevere,' he said roughly. 'You...make me unable to think. I cannot concentrate on anything else when you kiss me. How can I be expected to give the taxation system the proper amount of attention when all I can think about is taking you to bed?'

It was heady, having this power over him. In fact, it was surprising how much she liked it.

She smiled at him. 'I'm sure you'll think of something.'

His expression darkened. 'I do not appreciate you using sex to manipulate me.'

Sometimes she could tease him and sometimes she couldn't. Now was clearly one of the times she couldn't.

'I'm not trying to manipulate you,' she said, letting her smile fade to show him how serious she was. 'Marriage is a two-way street. This whole time it's been about you, and now I want something for me. I want to feel like a wife, not a mistress.'

'You already are a wife.'

'Yes, but you don't treat me like one,' she said firmly. 'I'm not your partner—I'm your comfort object. Your toy. You play with me when you feel like it, then put me away when you're done. I'm tired of it, Tiberius. You were the one who wanted to marry me, so I married you. Now I'm saying I want our marriage to be more than sex at night and public appearances.'

His gaze was fierce, his temper flaming, but she only stared back at him.

She wasn't afraid of him and she wasn't afraid of his temper. He would never do anything to hurt her, never do anything she didn't want. She knew that. In fact, the thing she was perhaps a little anxious about was that he might do something she *did* want—in which case her determination not to give in on this point might be undermined.

But he didn't move. Then like a door being shut on a fire, the heat in his gaze vanished, the light, crystalline grey becoming frosty.

'Very well,' he said, his tone as cool as his gaze. 'Perhaps we can discuss this during your instruction.'

Then, before she could say another word, he turned on his heel and went out.

CHAPTER NINE

TIBERIUS WENT TO his taxation meeting angry, and as he'd feared he found it difficult to concentrate. His body refused to go back to sleep, his hunger for his wife invading his every thought. He couldn't let his mind wander—not even for a second. Because if he did, it would return to the feel of her against him, the warmth of her hips beneath his palms. The soft brush of her mouth against his.

The determination in her blue eyes as she refused him.

He was beginning to both love and hate that determination of hers.

Love it because she was stubborn, and there was a strength in her that he found both fascinating and devastatingly attractive.

Hate it because he couldn't argue with her about the way he was treating her.

He *was* using her like a mistress or a toy. Coming to her at night, hungry and desperate for the sweet oblivion only she could give him, and then falling asleep in her arms. He'd never slept so well as in the past couple of weeks with her. But he always woke before she did, and then he'd leave the bed, driven by his need to keep progressing with his country's rebuild.

She wanted more than that from him. And, given the terrible childhood she'd suffered at the hands of her father and brothers, she deserved more. But he wasn't sure he could give her more. There was only so much of him to go around, and Kasimir needed him more than she did.

Still, her denial shouldn't have put him in such a vile temper. It was only sex, and he'd always been able to control his urges with ease. Except he was still furious about it. And he wasn't sure why.

Maybe it was about her demanding his time to teach her about being a queen—time he could ill afford. Then again, he hadn't liked the idea of someone else handling it. What she'd said about it being in his interest to do the teaching himself made sense—really, who better to teach her about being a queen than her king?

You like the idea. Admit it.

That was true. The idea of teaching her, spending a couple of hours a day in her presence that weren't about sex was…attractive. And he was curious about what kind of queen she would make. He had his own ideas about that, but he wanted to see if he was right.

He thought about it all evening, and as usual went to bed late that night, his body already waking, coming to aching, hungry life in anticipation of the pleasure to come.

But when he pushed open the door to his bedroom there was no sweet scent lingering in the air, and no warm, silky little body in his bed.

It was clear that she had gone elsewhere to sleep, and though he told himself it was her right, and that he wouldn't go searching for her, it was hours before he finally slept. Even giving himself relief didn't help. It was as if some part of him was still hungry for her. A part that had nothing to do with his need for sex. A part that wanted more.

The next morning he rose at dawn and spent yet another day in meetings, still trying and failing to get his new wife out of his head.

At midday an aide approached him with a message from the Queen, reminding him that he'd promised to give her a couple of hours of his time and that she'd be waiting for him in the orchard that afternoon.

He had no idea why she'd chosen the orchard, and knew he'd made her no such promises, yet when the hour approached he found himself watching the clock, felt his body gathering itself in anticipation, his heartbeat accelerating.

Ludicrous to feel this way about a meeting with his wife. And yet no matter how ludicrous he told himself it was, that didn't stop his excitement from building. Or stop him from excusing himself when the time came with far more alacrity that he should have.

He made his way quickly to the orchard—it was a gorgeous, sun-drenched day—and found her sitting under the orange tree he'd pushed her against the week before, on a rug spread out over the grass. She was in one of her pretty dresses, this one loose and floaty, the colour of fresh lavender. The front of her blonde curls had been tied back, the rest flowing down her back, and she looked so lovely and delicate and fairy-like that his heart almost stopped beating.

She was in the process of laying out food from a basket, and when she sensed his presence she looked up and gave him the sunniest, most devastatingly pretty smile. His heart, in fact, did stop.

'I hope you're hungry,' she said. 'I had the kitchen put together some afternoon tea for a picnic.'

His muscles tensed and he felt obscurely angry for some reason—as if her sitting there, pretty as a picture, with a delicious picnic all around her, was an affront. Maybe it was. Because, deep inside him, the part of him that had missed her the night before wanted nothing more than to sit on the rug and enjoy her picnic.

But he couldn't. It felt wrong. His mother hadn't died for him so that he could sit in the sun without a care in the world, and neither had his father. There was too much work to be done.

'Come and sit down,' she invited when he didn't move. 'Would you like some coffee? Or maybe a glass of champagne?'

'A picnic is not—'

'A picnic,' she interrupted calmly, 'is exactly what you need. I promise this will take no more than two hours, and if you're going to be teaching me all about being a queen then it won't matter if we sit in the sun with a picnic. You'd have to spend that two hours with me somewhere, hmm?'

He couldn't argue with that, so he found himself moving over to the rug and sitting down on it, watching her put some sandwiches on a plate and then leaning over to put it on the rug beside him.

'Why here?' he asked shortly as she piled food onto a second plate. 'My study would be more appropriate.'

'More appropriate, yes, but I'm tired of being inside.' She twinkled at him. 'It's much nicer being outside in the sun and the fresh air, don't you think? Especially when you've been cooped up inside all day.'

He wanted to deny it, but that was difficult when the sun shining down was warm on the back of his neck and the air was full of the smell of warm grass and oranges and the cool tang of the mountains around them.

Letting out a breath, he picked up a sandwich from the plate and began to eat, because he was actually quite hungry. 'Where were you last night?' he asked, even though he'd told himself he wasn't going to and that he didn't care.

'I felt like some time to myself,' she said. 'I didn't think it would matter to you if I wasn't there.'

'It didn't,' he replied, knowing it was a lie even as he said it. 'I only wanted to know where you were.'

She regarded him for a moment, her blue gaze assessing. 'I slept in the little room. You could have come to find me.'

Tiberius finished the sandwich, then picked up another. 'It was late. I didn't want to wake you.'

'Okay.' She ate her sandwich in tiny bites, and his gaze was drawn to the softness of her mouth and her small white teeth as she bit into the bread.

'You will be there tonight.' He'd meant it to sound like a question and instead it came out as a command.

'Will I?' She popped the rest of the sandwich into her mouth and chewed thoughtfully. 'That will depend on whether you're going to treat me as a wife or a toy.'

This again. Annoyance twisted inside him. 'I am treating you as a wife.'

'No, you're not. A husband and wife generally spend time together, and we do not.'

'Because we're the rulers of a nation. Our marriage will not be like other people's.'

She gave him a level look. 'And if I want it to be?'

Everything in him drew tight. 'What are you saying?'

'I'm saying that I want our marriage to be more, Tiberius. Like I told you yesterday, I want it to be more than just sleeping together at night.'

Tension crawled through him, though he wasn't sure why. 'It is more. You wear my ring, you are at my side, you are my queen.'

'That is not a relationship, and a relationship is what I want. And not one based entirely on sex. I don't think that's too much to ask for, especially if and when we decide to have children.' One fair brow arched. 'Or do you really want your children to have the kind of upbringing you did?'

That washed over him like a cold shock. He hadn't spared a thought for children beyond knowing that he'd need heirs, and he certainly hadn't thought about what kind of childhood he wanted for them.

One like yours? Crushed under the weight of other people's expectations?

His chest grew tight with instinctive denial. 'No,' he said tersely. 'I do not want that.'

'Good. Then we agree on one thing, at least.' She leaned forward and reached for the bottle of champagne sitting in the basket. 'Let's have a toast.'

'We should be discussing what you need to do as queen,' he growled. 'Not drinking in the sun and talking about children.'

She only shrugged and uncorked the bottle with a deft movement. 'Okay, then. Let's talk about me being a queen.'

She handed him a glass, which he had no choice but to take, then she poured some sparkling liquid into it before doing the same for herself. Putting the bottle down, she picked up her glass and knocked it gently against his.

'To the future.'

Then she lifted it to drink, and somehow managed to spill nearly all of it down the front of her pretty dress.

Tiberius sat there, unable to move, his gaze pinned to the wet fabric and the way it stuck to her skin, clinging to the curves of her breasts, making it very clear that she wasn't wearing a bra.

'Oh, no…' She put down her glass and looked at him wide-eyed. 'I'm all wet.'

He was suddenly painfully hard, with visions of himself peeling the damp silk from her and licking the champagne from her skin before checking to see just how wet she really was reeling through his brain.

Her deep blue gaze met his, and he knew that she could read the desire in his eyes because her own leapt to meet it.

'This is a seduction, isn't it?' he asked roughly.

'Is it?'

She made no move to dry herself, sitting there with the silk clinging to her, making it clear that her nipples were hard.

'I'm already seduced. You don't need to do this now. Couldn't it wait until tonight?'

'We're talking about you teaching me how to be a queen, Tiberius. Nothing else.'

Except she wasn't looking at him that way, and before he quite knew what he was doing he'd reached out, hauling her into his lap so she was facing him, her legs on either side of his hips.

'Time for your first lesson, then,' he said and lifting his hands, plunged them into her hair and took her mouth like he owned it.

It was reckless to do this out in the open, but Guinevere had decided that Tiberius wasn't the only master strategist. She was one too. She'd organised the picnic with the kitchen, then given instructions to both the staff and the palace guards that the orchard was to be out of bounds for the next couple of hours.

She'd wondered if he'd even come, but when his tall figure had come striding through the trees her heart had leapt. He'd looked devastatingly attractive, in dark trousers and a black shirt, and it had been all she could do not to lay hands on him the moment he'd sat down.

He'd missed her the night before—she could see it in his face, hear it in his voice. If it truly hadn't mattered to him then he wouldn't have asked, but he had. And the truth was she'd missed him too. It had taken all her of considerable will to stay in the library the night before, to deny him the pleasure of her body. But this was part of the lesson she wanted to teach him—that he couldn't have everything his own way—and that was a difficult lesson for a man like him.

Nevertheless, he had to learn. He had to understand that he could have moments for himself. That life wasn't all about work or the burden of kingship. That there could be moments of joy and happiness.

She wasn't sure when his wellbeing had come to matter to her so much, but it had, and so here, in the sunlight of the orchard, on a beautiful day, she'd spread before him a picnic and determined that for a couple of hours he could relax.

Then she'd thought that maybe that relaxation should be physical. They weren't in bed, for a change, and maybe in the sun, after some pleasure, he'd lose some of the tension she could sense in the air around him.

She probably needn't have indulged in the performance of spilling perfectly good champagne over herself, but she'd wanted him to be hungry for her. She'd wanted him to forget everything but her.

And certainly the wet fabric of her dress was doing that work for her.

The flare of desire in his eyes had been the only warning she'd had before he'd leaned forward and dragged her into his lap.

Now she didn't pull away from his hungry kiss, pressing her body to his instead, and kissing him back just as hungrily.

The feral growl he made in the back of his throat delighted her, and she wasn't displeased when he ripped apart the thin silk of her dress. He put one hand between her shoulder blades to support her as he bent her back, pulling the fabric aside, kissing his way down her throat, over her collarbones to her breasts, still damp with champagne. She gasped as pleasure lanced through her. His mouth had found one of her nipples and was drawing hard on it.

His free hand tugged at more of the dress fabric, ripping it all the way down so that there was nothing between them but his clothing and the little lacy pair of knickers she wore beneath the dress.

His arms came around her, supporting her as he bent her back further, his mouth resting in the hollow of her throat as he shifted one hand down between her thighs, stroking her, making pleasure ripple everywhere.

She sighed, giving herself up to him, to the movement of his hands and the way he kissed and tasted her body, hot and hungry. But he often took the lead in the bedroom, and while she enjoyed that very much, since her experience was limited, she was starting to get more confident.

This was about him, and she wanted to give to him as much as he gave to her.

So she took his hands and held them still. 'Let me,' she murmured. 'Let me give you pleasure, Your Majesty.'

He stilled, his gaze full of flames. He was such an intense man and he felt things so deeply, she could see it. It was his love for his country that drove him, but maybe there was also something else. Something deeper. She wanted to know what it was, what motor kept driving him on. And perhaps if she gave him some release he'd tell her.

She lifted her hands to his face and cupped it gently between her palms, then she leaned in and began to kiss him…butterfly-light kisses on his forehead, the strong bridge of his nose, his eyelids, his cheekbones. Raining down soft, tender kisses that ended with the brush of her lips against his.

'No,' he murmured in protest. 'I need you now, lioness.'

'And you can have me. Just be patient.'

She kept on kissing his face, then his throat, her hands moving to the buttons of his shirt and undoing them. Then she was stroking his chest, tracing the hard muscle beneath his satiny skin, worshipping him.

'Guinevere,' he growled in warning as her hands strayed to his stomach, and then further, flicking open the button of his trousers and then the zip, sliding her hand beneath the cotton of his underwear and finding him long and thick and hard.

'*Guinevere,*' he said again, his voice guttural.

'Shh…' she murmured, stroking him gently, tracing the length of him with her fingers. She kissed his mouth as she did so, tasting him lightly. A tender kiss, slowly— very slowly—deepening into something sweeter and hotter.

He made a sound deep in his throat, but he didn't move. He'd gone very still, and she could feel the tension in his muscles. But it wasn't denial. It was almost as if he'd never felt like this before and wasn't sure what to do.

And perhaps he hadn't. Had anyone ever been tender with him? Had anyone ever been soft? Had anyone ever touched him as if he was beautiful, a work of art you had to be careful with?

His breathing was fast, and normally that was a sign that he'd take charge, put her on her back and thrust inside her. Yet he remained still. As if he was waiting.

She reached down between them, slipping aside her underwear, then gripped him and positioned him before raising herself slightly, easing down, feeling the delicious glide of him as he slid inside her.

'Guinevere,' he whispered again, his voice roughened and yet soft. But it wasn't a warning this time. It was something else. Something that held a note that made her heart tighten in response.

She looked into his beautiful face, met the glorious silver blaze in his eyes. And then she moved, watching the flames in his eyes burn higher and higher. Kissing him tenderly and gently, she let her hands stroke his shoulders and his chest, loving the feel of him. Surrounding herself with him.

The pleasure grew, building high and hot, and there was an urgency to it but also a gentleness, and a sweetness that made her want to stay like this for ever. Then, just as it began to get too much for her, he slipped his hand between her thighs, down to where they were joined, and stroked her. At the same time his other hand settled heavily into the small of her back, holding her to him.

The pleasure broke, exploding slowly and beautifully like a firework, a peaceful, inexorable tide that made them both shake before touching down lightly back to earth.

She put her head against his shoulder, leaning bonelessly against him as his hand cupped the back of her head, his thumb moving gently over the curve of her skull.

He didn't speak, and neither did she, both of them content to sit in the small bubble of peace they'd created for themselves. And beneath her hands she felt the hard muscles of his shoulders and chest finally relax.

'I can't help feeling,' he said, his voice deep and rough with the after-effects of their passion, 'that I have been expertly seduced by my own wife.'

She smiled against his shoulder. 'Yes, you have. And I'll have you know I'm quite pleased with myself.'

'So you should be.' His hand slid down to the back of her neck, stroking her idly. 'I'm sorry about your pretty dress. I will get you another.'

'I don't care.' She peeked up at him. 'It sacrificed itself for a good cause.'

He glanced down and smiled, his gaze sparking with something that wasn't physical desire, yet had elements of it. And also elements of something warm and tender and utterly glorious.

Her heart tightened painfully, and a kind of wonder moved through her that he'd chosen to give such a smile to her.

'I'll buy you many sacrificial victims, in that case,' he said. 'You can offer one up to me every evening.'

'Please do.'

She sighed, then moved, shifting herself off him and

wrapping the remains of her dress around her. He made a growl of protest, reaching for her to pull her down with him as he lay on his back on the rug. She propped her head up with her hand and she leaned an elbow on his chest.

'Did you really spend all your childhood learning how to be a king?' she asked idly—though the question wasn't idle in the slightest. She was taking advantage of his relaxation.

'Yes,' he said. 'My father knew it would take time to get the throne back, so he had to start early. He'd initially planned to take it back himself, but then he got sick.'

'So you had to be the one, then?' She picked up an olive from the bowl nearby and fed it to him. 'That must have been difficult.'

'It was. It took longer than we'd hoped, since getting support for our cause took some time.'

She thought for a moment, then picked up a grape and fed that to him. 'My father used to make fun of you. As a way to reduce the threat you presented, I think. He called you weak and ineffectual.'

There was a satisfied expression on Tiberius's face that she secretly thought looked far too good on him. 'I'm glad he did. It meant your father's supporters underestimated me.'

Guinevere picked up another olive and ate it, trying to decide what to ask him next. Something that wouldn't make him tense up or scare him away. But she burned to know so much.

'I'm sorry about your mother,' she said carefully. 'It must have been hard to grow up without her.'

'I was too young to remember her—and my father didn't talk much about her—but I certainly felt the lack when I was younger.'

She watched him, noting the shadows cast over his face by the sun and the branches of the tree above them. Gilding the long, sooty length of his lashes, highlighting the strong lines of his forehead and nose.

'My mother died young, too,' she said after a moment. 'And I don't remember her either.'

His gaze rested on hers and there was concern in his eyes. 'Did you have anyone, lioness? Anyone to care for you?'

A lump rose unexpectedly in her throat and she had to swallow hard because, again, this was supposed to be about him, not her. 'No. I was safer being alone.'

He reached out and brushed her cheek with his fingertips. 'I'm sorry you had to deal with that. But know that you're not alone now. And that you're not a prisoner here. You may leave the palace whenever you wish.'

She badly wanted him to tell her that she had him, but he didn't, and that made her heart clench unexpectedly.

'You know that you're not alone either, don't you?' she couldn't help saying, leaning into his touch. 'That I am here?'

His mouth curved and the warmth in it made the tightness in her heart clench into a strange kind of pain. 'And I'm glad of it. Speaking of which…shouldn't we be discussing your role as Queen?'

She smiled back. 'Yes. But have another olive first.'

He didn't protest when she fed it to him, nipping at her fingertips instead, and soon they were too distracted to discuss anything at all.

CHAPTER TEN

Tiberius glanced at his watch yet again, to check the time. It wasn't quite five, but it would be soon—though not soon enough for the anticipation gathering inside him.

At five a messenger would come and hand him a note, telling him where to meet his wife. He never knew where she was going to hold their daily two hours of queenship teaching—she always picked the place—but it came as a pleasant surprise every time.

They'd been doing this for a couple of weeks now, and while initially he'd been impatient for the two hours to end, after that first time—on the rug in the orchard, with her warm body against his, her touching him slowly and with care, then feeding him olives and grapes—now he was almost disappointed when it was over.

Those first few times they'd ended up getting distracted by sex—which he hadn't minded—and then, in the lazy aftermath, indulging in some idle conversation. He'd always hated small talk and meaningless discussion—it felt like a waste of time. Why talk pleasantries when there were important conversations to be had? But for some reason, after meeting with Guinevere, he found himself in no hurry to get back to the palace.

Their discussions ranged over books, art, science and politics. He started to enjoy their conversations. She was very knowledgeable about a host of different subjects, due to reading her way through the palace library. She was also curious, and interested in what he had to say, though his own knowledge of certain subjects was limited, given the narrowness of his upbringing.

She also met him in a variety of different places. First the orchard, then a clearing in the forest. One day it rained, so he met her in her little library, and then there was the time when the sky was bright blue and she met him by the pool. There were cocktails and delicious finger foods that time, then they'd swum—which had soon evolved into extremely hot sex, both of them slippery with water, on one of the sun loungers.

He'd begun to look forward to their meetings, begun to find the length of time he spent in other meetings an imposition. He had to be very stern with himself not to be distracted when he was working, but it was difficult.

He'd also started to look forward to their public appearances together, which he found a delight when she was by his side. She was beginning to win over those few stalwarts who didn't like her because she was an Accorsi, with her smile and the natural way she talked to people. Little girls in particular loved their new and pretty queen, and there was always a little posse of them waiting for Guinevere whenever they appeared together.

It wasn't all idle conversation, naturally. They discussed Kasimir, and her role as queen—though he'd soon discovered that she didn't need much in the way of instruction. Her natural empathy, her curiosity and quick wit had helped her pick up the subtleties of queenly duties with relative ease. She had initiative too. It had only been a few days before one of his aides had told him that the Queen was involving herself in various charities, as well as taking a special interest in health services.

She was a remarkable woman, and every day he found there were new aspects of her to respect and admire. Really, marrying her was turning out to be one of his better decisions.

At last, five came, and the door of the meeting room opened to admit the Queen's aide. The man came quickly over to Tiberius and handed him a note. Tiberius unfolded it.

Meet me on our bedroom balcony tonight. Seven p.m.

He was conscious of a slight disappointment that he'd have to wait another few hours—he'd never been good at waiting—but her choice of meeting place was intriguing. The balcony... Why on earth there?

He retired to his office, to finish looking through the endless pile of documents that required his signature, but couldn't concentrate.

In the end he found himself striding to the royal apartments to meet his queen a good ten minutes before she'd said.

There were still palace staff on the balcony when he arrived, laying out food on the stone table there, as tealight candles in glass holders cast a soft, flickering glow.

Guinevere, who'd been directing the staff, gave him

a surprised look as he appeared. 'Oh!' she exclaimed. 'You're early.'

She wore a light linen wrap dress of deep blue, her hair loose over her shoulder, and looked so unutterably lovely that he felt ravenous for her.

'I was impatient,' he said, dismissing the staff with a wave of his hand.

Once they'd gone, he crossed over to where Guinevere stood and took her hands in his.

'Why the balcony?'

She smiled. 'I thought you'd enjoy watching the sun set while you give me more instruction.'

The mention of 'instruction' made him hard, and that was strange. Because it wasn't as if they only had sex during these meetings. They also did it at night, in bed together. He most certainly wasn't abstinent.

She hadn't absented herself from his bed again, the way she had done that one night, so he couldn't fathom why the more time he spent with her, the more he wanted.

Somewhere in the depths of him a warning bell tolled, but he ignored it. This was purely a physical infatuation, nothing more, and as long as he continued to make progress with rebuilding his country, why shouldn't he enjoy more time with his wife?

'Also,' she added, threading her fingers through his and leading him over to the table, 'you need dinner.'

She was always feeding him. Not that he objected. It was just strange to have someone invested in his well-being. It wasn't that his aides weren't, but with them it wasn't about him, but his role as King. Guinevere, though, saw past his crown to the man he was behind it, and some part of him took deep satisfaction in that.

'This looks delicious,' he said as he sat down on the cushioned chair at the head of the table.

It was a long table, meant for more than two people, but instead of sitting opposite him, Guinevere sat beside him.

'I hope so.' She got a plate and began to serve him, as she always did at these meetings. 'I had the kitchen make all your favourites.'

Tiberius watched her. 'You know my favourites?'

'Of course.' She gave him a grin. 'I asked the staff what you liked and they told me.'

She has made an effort to know you, but what do you know of her?

What did he know?

He knew she was curious and passionate. That she was empathic and intelligent. That her childhood had been awful and yet it hadn't turned her into a terrible person. She'd been quiet and terrified when he'd first met her, but she'd blossomed since, revealing the warm, generous and caring woman she was beneath the fear. Clearly she was thriving in her new role.

There were many things he knew about her...more than he'd realised.

'I should be doing this for you,' he said as she handed him the plate. 'You are spoiling me, lioness.'

She lifted a shoulder as she began getting food for herself. 'I enjoy spoiling you,' she said, flashing him a smile. 'You deserve to be spoiled.'

Do you?

The thought came out of nowhere, and he felt as if a chill breeze had moved over his skin. He ignored it. It didn't matter what he did or didn't deserve. She'd chosen to do these little things for him, and he wouldn't hurt her by rejecting them.

What about what she deserves?

She deserved much—which he'd give her when he had time for it. Besides, it wasn't as if he didn't do anything for her. Every night he made her scream with the pleasure he gave her, and that wasn't nothing.

'Tell me about your day,' she said, as she did every time they met.

So while they ate he told her about what he and his aides had discussed that day, and about the current issues they were facing, as well as the ones they'd have to deal with in the near future.

'I'm going to get my events team to organise a national tour,' he said after they'd eaten. 'But before that we have an international meeting to attend in Geneva.'

Guinevere put an elbow on the table and leaned her chin in her hand. '"We"?'

'Of course, "we". You will naturally be by my side.'

Her cheeks went pink, and she gave him another of her heartbreaking smiles. 'Oh, that sounds amazing. Have you been there before?'

He had, and told her so, and they discussed travelling for a bit before he asked her how her day had gone. He always asked, and he always found it interesting. In fact, he was starting to find everything about her interesting.

After they'd watched the sunset on the balcony,

Guinevere took his hand and led him inside, telling him she had a surprise for him.

It was full dark by the time they stepped outside the palace, following the path to the orchard once more. There, Guinevere put a rug down on the grass and pulled him down to sit beside her.

'What is this all about?' he asked, as she lay on her back on the rug.

She was smiling as she patted the rug beside her. 'Lie down and I'll tell you.'

So he did, lying on his back, watching the stars wheeling above their heads.

'I want you to tell me about the stars, Tiberius,' she said.

He realised what she'd done then. She'd taken him back to his boyhood, to those stolen moments of quiet and peace when he hadn't been the saviour of a country, but only a boy. A boy who was part of something greater…the entire living universe.

Something inside him relaxed in that moment… something that had been tense for a long time. Strangely, it felt as if he hadn't been able to breathe properly, but now, right here, he could draw a full breath for the first time.

The stars glittered in the black velvet of the sky and he lifted a hand, pointing out the different constellations, feeling memories of his childhood interest in astronomy flooding back.

She nestled against him, her voice full of wonder as she asked him questions and then listened to him talk, and he realised that for the first time since he could remember he was utterly relaxed. Content to be in this moment. The relentless engine inside him finally still.

Guinevere lay with her head pillowed on Tiberius's shoulder, listening to him talk about the stars. He knew a great deal about them, and for a change he talked without the edge of impatience that usually coloured his voice.

There was no tension in him, she could feel it in his body. And that made her feel good in turn, that she'd managed to give him this. Two hours of every day when he didn't have to be a king, where he could be free of his burdens if only for a little time.

He needed it. And perhaps the worst part about it was that he didn't even know he needed it, that she'd had to give him these hours by stealth.

After the first couple of days she'd wondered if he'd realise what she was doing, and perhaps stop coming, but he didn't. And if he did indeed understand what she was doing, he certainly didn't question it.

One thing was sure, though. She loved organising their meetings. Loved choosing places to have them—places he'd enjoy—and choosing food too, since he often forgot to eat, or so the palace staff told her. She loved spending time with him, talking with him. He was an interesting and highly intelligent man. He told her all about his plans for Kasimir—how he hoped to develop certain aspects of it for carefully managed tourism and also create export opportunities for Kasimiran products.

It was clear that he loved his people, loved his country, and that his whole life was directed to one purpose.

Making things better. And that desire to make things better, to protect his people, came from a deep empathy, she could tell.

An empathy that came from the man rather than the King.

She wanted to know more about that man, that person, rather than about the role he played, so often their conversations would stray onto other topics as she tried to draw out of him glimpses of who he was deep down.

She discovered that he liked good food, and enjoyed wine, but that he had no hobbies. His interests were entirely bent to one purpose. Being a king. She needed to find out more, she decided, which was why today she'd organised to meet him later at night, so that after dinner they could lie in the grass and watch the stars, the way he'd done as a boy.

And she decided that there was nothing nicer than lying here next to him, listening to his deep voice telling her about the rings of Saturn, and how far away the moon was, and other such things.

'Next time I'll bring a telescope,' she said. 'So you can show me some of the planets.'

'I'll get one of my staff to find one.'

They lay in companionable silence for a moment, then he said, 'Why did you bring me out here?'

She let out a breath, debating whether or not to tell him the truth. 'I wanted to remind you that there was more to life than being a king,' she said at last—because why not tell him the truth? He should hear it. 'You said that those moments when you were a boy, looking up at the stars, were the most peaceful you ever had, and

I just…wanted to give you that and to remind you what it felt like.'

He said nothing for a long moment. 'Thank you,' he murmured eventually. 'It's been a…long time since I've done anything like this.'

She turned her head, looking up at his face, all silver light and shadows under the moon. 'Why, Tiberius? Why do you drive yourself so hard?'

'Because there is a lot at stake.' His voice wasn't impatient for a change, but almost meditative. 'Because it's taking far too long for me to change things.' There was another pause, then he added, 'Because my mother died to protect me. Instead of saving her, my father had to leave her behind in order to save me. She insisted, apparently.'

Guinevere's heart clenched in her chest. 'And your father?'

'Before he died of cancer, five years ago, he made me promise that I would dedicate my life to claiming back the crown and rebuilding what your father broke.'

'What about you?' She asked the question almost hesitantly. 'Is that something you want to do?'

'It isn't a question of what I want,' he said simply. 'It is what I have to do. It's the right thing to do.'

Was that regret in his tone? She couldn't tell.

'Did you never want to do something else?'

He was looking up at the sky, the expression on his face unreadable. 'No,' he said. 'When I was a child I wanted to be an astronaut—like every other little boy, no doubt. But that wasn't my destiny.'

The pain in her heart seemed to deepen. There was

no wistfulness in his voice, only a flat note that excluded any possibility of him wanting to be anything other than what he was.

'So you were told very early on what you had to be?' she said.

'Yes. From the age of ten I knew that that one day I would be King.'

'Did you ever…wish for it to be different?'

He turned his head, looking down at her. 'Different? What do you mean?'

'Did you ever wish that you weren't heir to the throne, I mean?'

He looked thoughtful. 'I don't remember,' he said at last. 'I don't remember ever having the choice—not that I would have chosen any differently if I had.' Something flickered in his eyes then that she couldn't read. 'My mother died to save me. She sacrificed herself and I have to make that sacrifice mean something. The same for my father too. On his death bed he made me swear that I would reclaim the crown and be a good king for Kasimir.'

She'd told him what a terrible burden she thought that was before, and she still believed it. That the purpose of his entire life was to make his parents' deaths mean something seemed a terrible burden to have to carry.

'You can make their deaths mean something and not drive yourself into an early grave,' she said. 'And you can allow yourself other interests that have nothing to do with being a king.'

His gaze flicked back to hers. 'Speak plainly, lioness. What is it you're trying to say?'

She paused for a moment, debating the wisdom of discussing this with him again. But she had to try and make him understand—for both their sakes.

'You're working too hard, Tiberius,' she said at last. 'You're not allowing yourself any time off or even time out. If you burn yourself out you'll no longer be able to do much of anything.'

'Why don't you let me be the judge of that, hmm?'

Guinevere held his darkened silver gaze. 'You're not going to disappoint them, Tiberius. You do know that, don't you?'

He frowned. 'Disappoint who?'

'Your parents. They put a lot of expectations on you, didn't they?'

'No more than any other parent. And no more than was necessary.' He eased her head off his shoulder gently and sat up. 'Being King is a high-pressure role—so, yes, of course the expectations will end up being heavy.'

That edge was back in his voice again, and she could have kicked herself for making things awkward. That wasn't what tonight was supposed to be about.

She shouldn't have asked difficult questions, shouldn't she?

'I understand,' she said quickly. 'And I'm not attacking them or criticising them. I just want you to know that you don't have to be strong all the time...that you don't have to push yourself constantly.'

'You're very invested in my wellbeing.'

'Of course I am. I'm your wife and you matter to me.' The words came out sounding a lot more emphatic than they should have. A lot more.

He stared at her, studying her face as if it was map he was trying to read. 'Guinevere,' he said at last. 'Our marriage is not like other people's, remember?'

She frowned, not understanding. 'What? What do you mean?'

'I mean,' he went on gently, 'that we did not marry for love.'

'I know that,' she said, unsure why the declaration should hurt. 'What has that got to do with you mattering to me?'

'I don't want you to expect things from me that you will never get. For example, you also matter to me—but not more than Kasimir. The country always comes first.'

It was the answer she'd expected, and yet the moment he said it the hurt inside her grew a little more, cut a little deeper.

'I know that,' she said reflexively. 'I'm not asking you to put me ahead of the country.'

'No, I can see you're not. I just need you to know that should you want more from me, you will never get it—understand?'

She wanted to ask him what he meant by 'more', but she had a horrible feeling she knew already. Love. That was what he meant, wasn't it? Love would never be a part of their marriage, because he was already in love with Kasimir.

You can't ask him to put you ahead of the country.

No, she couldn't. She could never be that selfish. Yet a part of her desperately wished she could.

Why? Why does he matter so much?

But she thought she knew the answer to that already.

It was an answer that had been steadily forming itself deep in her heart for the past three weeks. That grew every time she spent time with him…every time he held her in his arms. That wanted more and more of him until she knew that nothing would ever be enough. That had her dreaming of him, and staring at him, and had her heart beating fast whenever they met.

You're falling in love with him.

Of course she was, and she hadn't known because it had never happened to her before. Nevertheless, she knew what this powerful current was, a tide that responded to him as if he was the moon and she the sea, rushing in when he was here, only to retreat when he wasn't.

It was love.

She was in love with her husband.

CHAPTER ELEVEN

THE BALLROOM WAS full of people. Royalty and nobility from other European nations, as well as heads of state. Music played, and the interior of the old castle on Lake Geneva, where the international meeting was being held, lit up.

Tiberius had had a satisfactory few days, meeting with other leaders, making valuable political alliances. He and Guinevere were due to fly back to Kasimir the next day, and he was almost sorry about it.

Not far from where he stood, chatting with some other leaders, was Guinevere, resplendent in a ballgown of pale silvery-blue silk. It was strapless, revealing her slender shoulders and pale throat, the fabric cupping her breasts lovingly. Her curls were piled on her head with a few loose, artfully tumbling around her ears, held in place with a couple of diamond combs that glittered and sparkled in the light.

He'd given her the necklace she wore of pale sapphires and diamonds, circling the slender column of her throat, and that glittered too. She seemed even more fairy-like tonight, sparkling like a delicate snow crystal in the lights of the ballroom.

He watched her, unable to take his gaze from her.

She needed a tiara, he decided. Many of other ladies present were wearing one, and after all she was a queen, even if she hadn't been formally crowned.

For the past two weeks he'd been thinking and thinking about what he could do for her—something as special as what she'd given him in those two hours he reserved for her every day. Those two hours that he'd begun to crave more and more with every day that passed. They were special, those hours. They were sacrosanct. And he'd even begun to wonder if he could afford to stretch them to three.

He wanted to reciprocate—show her that he appreciated what she did for him, that he admired and respected her, that she was everything he'd ever wanted in a queen and more. But he hadn't thought of the perfect thing…until now.

A coronation—that's what she should have. He didn't care that his own had been perfunctory, but for her… She should be feted. She should have all the attention she deserved. His fairy princess should be made into a queen with all the pomp and ceremony at his disposal.

It would be a good thing too, for the people. A happy event to boost their spirits after the long years of Accorsi rule. He would decree a public holiday and Guinevere would be crowned in the cathedral in the central city.

He watched as she laughed at something someone had said to her, her smile lighting up her face, making her even more lovely than she was already.

Yes, she should wear a silver gown, or pale gold, and she would look impossibly beautiful in the Kasimiran

Queen's crown, all diamonds and sapphires. He would invite the world's media, livestream the whole thing to the rest of the globe. It would be a major event and she would finally get all the attention she deserved.

Impatient to tell her of his plans, he moved over to where she stood, slipping an arm around her waist and drawing her close. 'Spare me five minutes, my queen,' he murmured in her ear.

She glanced up at him, smiling, and his chest tightened. Her smiles were truly the loveliest he'd ever seen.

'As long as it's only five,' she said, teasing, before excusing herself from the little group she'd been chatting with.

'What is it?' she asked, as he drew her over to one of the windows that overlooked the magnificent lake.

'I have an idea,' he said. 'You've been such a delight over the past couple of weeks, and I've been very remiss as a husband. I have not given you anything in return.'

'You've given me your time, Tiberius,' she said. 'That's the most important thing. That's all I need.'

'But you deserve more, little lioness. So much more.' He took her hands in his and held them. 'I'd like to hold a formal coronation for you. In the cathedral. With the world's media looking on, and naturally all our people. A symbol of what our union and you being queen means to Kasimir.'

Her smile flickered momentarily, though he wasn't sure what that meant. 'A coronation? I don't need a coronation, Tiberius.'

'Perhaps not, but I'd like you to have one all the same.

Don't you think our people and the world should see the lovely woman who is Queen of Kasimir?'

She squeezed his fingers, then let them go. 'They already know who I am. Besides, it's a lot of money to spend. Money that could better be spent on the hospital, for example.'

Irritation caught at him. This was not the response he'd expected, he had to admit. He'd thought she'd be pleased, at the very least.

'The people could do with a happy event.' He tried to keep the annoyance from his voice. 'And I will decree a public holiday, which should boost morale even further. It will be for them, not just you.'

Her smile seemed strained now. 'Oh. That does sound like it could be something...worthwhile, then.'

They were in a crowded ballroom, and he didn't particularly want to cause a scene, but her muted reaction had got under his skin.

'You don't like the idea?' he asked, trying to keep his voice level. 'I wanted to do something nice for you.'

Her lashes fell, veiling her gaze. 'If you want to do something nice for me, you could give me another hour of your time. It doesn't need to be anything else.'

Instantly he felt defensive. 'This will be for our people, Guinevere.'

Her lashes rose again, her blue gaze meeting his. 'So it's not really for me at all, is it?'

A curious anger was growing in him—part defensiveness, part disappointment and part an odd pain that his suggestion had been rejected. Yet it seemed ridiculous to be so angry about that. Why should he care?

'Of course it is,' he said curtly. 'But it will help our people also.'

'So you'd rather organise a hugely expensive coronation for me than give me another hour of your time. Is that what you're saying?'

Frustration joined the mix of emotions inside him. He had no more time to give, and she should understand that. 'Why is that a problem?'

Her blue gaze darkened, her smile just a memory. 'You don't understand, do you? That I might enjoy spending time with you and want more of it.'

'We've talked about this,' he said, trying to mask his impatience. 'Kasimir is the most—'

'Important thing. Yes, I know,' she interrupted, the blue sparks of her temper beginning to show. 'But it's possible to do both, Tiberius. You can rule your country and be a husband at the same time.' She gestured at the crowded ballroom. 'There are plenty of people here who are great examples of that.'

His anger built and he was conscious of it being out of proportion to what she'd actually said, and yet he seemed to be powerless to ignore it.

'Those people do not have the same history we do,' he said through gritted teeth. 'And neither do their countries.'

Guinevere's gaze came back to his. 'You mean me being the daughter of your enemy?'

'No,' he snapped, forgetting himself. 'Our marriage being one of convenience.'

'Yes, until you made it real.' She turned to face him

fully now, standing small and indomitable before him. 'You were the one who didn't want a divorce, Tiberius.'

'And you agreed,' he shot back.

She looked away abruptly, her hands clasped in front of her now, a sure sign of her distress.

You are ruining this for her.

Pain threaded through him at the sight of her small hands, holding on to each other so tightly. It was a pain he didn't understand. Because it hurt him that she was distressed. It hurt him to think that he was ruining this evening for her, too, especially when he'd been trying to make things better.

'Little lioness,' he said softly, taking her hands once more and drawing her behind one of the columns. 'I don't want to fight with you. If you don't want a coronation, then we won't have one. I only thought you'd like it.'

She stared up at him, her gaze luminous, and much to his shock he saw tears in her eyes.

'Guinevere?' He drew her closer. 'What's wrong?'

'It's not the coronation,' she said after a moment, her voice thick and shaky. 'I don't…don't need any of that. What I need is you, Tiberius. More of your time, more of your company, just…more of you.'

'Lioness,' he murmured, tightening his grip. 'You know I can't—'

'I need it because I'm in love with you.'

The stunned look on his face told her everything she needed to know about how he felt. There was no joy, no happiness. Only shock.

She'd known it would be a difficult thing to tell him, but she hadn't been able to mask her feelings about his coronation offer well enough. His offer to do something for her, that she'd hoped would be about spending more time with her, only for it to be about a coronation had been too sharp a disappointment.

It wasn't that she didn't appreciate it, it was that the thing he'd chosen wasn't really about her at all. It was about what she represented as his wife, his queen, and their marriage as a symbolic union for all of Kasimir.

It wasn't about her.

It wasn't about Guinevere, who was in love with her husband and who only wanted to spend time with him.

But of course time was his most precious commodity, and he didn't have enough of it to spare for her and her alone.

She shouldn't have told him the real reason for her disappointment, but not telling him the truth would only cause more trouble between them, especially when she wasn't good at hiding her feelings.

But she'd said it now, the the truth that had been sitting there all this time since that moment under the stars in the orchard.

She loved him, and over the past two weeks spending more time with him, and now coming to Switzerland, had only made it more clear to her. She loved being with him, talking to him, arguing with him, having him at her side whenever they were in public and then being held in his arms at night in their bed.

She loved him and she didn't know what to do. Because while she'd realised she was in love with him that night, he'd made it very clear that love would not be a part of this marriage. That Kasimir would always come first and there was no room in his heart for anything else.

There was no room in his heart for her.

He was a king, and his first responsibility was to his country. Not her.

She could give him an ultimatum—tell him she was leaving him if he didn't put her first, but that was something she'd never do. It would force him into an impossible position and that felt terribly unfair.

'I'm sorry,' she murmured, pulling her hands from his. 'I know that's not what you want to hear. I'm sorry. I shouldn't have said it.'

Slowly the shock ebbed from his expression, leaving his eyes hard, cold chips of diamond. 'Guinevere. That is not what our marriage is about—you know that.'

Her throat felt tight. 'Yes, I know,' she forced out. 'Don't worry, I'm not going to ask you for anything. I only wanted you to know that that's how I feel.'

'It's not something I'll ever be able to reciprocate.' Now his voice sounded hard too. 'You know why.'

'Yes.' She couldn't quite mask her bitterness. 'You have to sacrifice yourself on Kasimir's altar and that of your parents' deaths.'

Anger leaped in his eyes, as she had known it would since it had been a terrible thing for her to say.

'Their deaths have nothing to do with this.'

She shouldn't argue. They were in a public ballroom, for God's sake. And yet she couldn't stop the words that spilled from her. 'Don't they, though? Isn't that why you can't afford to take your eye off the crown? Not even for a moment? You're so desperate to prove you're worth your mother's sacrifice—and your father's too.'

His expression became forbidding. 'How is that wrong?' he demanded. 'She died protecting me and my father sacrificed his wife for me. Shouldn't I prove to them that they didn't die for nothing?'

At that, her eyes filled with tears. 'You've already proved that, Tiberius. You've reclaimed the crown and you're getting Kasimir back on track. You have some wonderful plans for the future. And they're gone now. What more do you need to prove?'

Tension had begun to roll off him like a wave. 'Everything,' he said harshly. 'My father was clear that a king couldn't have anything else in his life but his country… that anything else was a distraction. And that doesn't end simply because I have a wife and a family.'

She blinked, her throat getting tight. 'There should be room in your life for happiness as well, Tiberius. There should be room in your life for love. Don't you think that's what your mother would have wanted?'

'You know nothing about what my mother would have wanted.'

'No,' she said softly. 'But neither do you. I'm sure she would want what's best for you, and running yourself into the ground for a country that doesn't care about you isn't it.'

'So what are you saying? That I give up everything? Give up the crown I worked for so long to claim just for you?'

That hurt, as he must know it would.

'No, that's not what I'm saying.' She pulled her hands from his, swallowing past the unbearable tightness in her throat. 'You're a king, but don't forget you're also a man, and one doesn't cancel out the other. How can a king make his people happy if he doesn't even know what happiness feels like?'

His expression shuttered. 'I don't need to know. Happiness is irrelevant.'

'It's not,' she said, unable to stop a tear from sliding down her cheek. 'It's important, and it's only been in the past couple of weeks with you that I've realised how important.'

But he ignored her, glancing down at his watch. 'I'm sorry, Guinevere. But this is a pointless discussion. I suggest we have it at a later date, and not in such a public place.'

He was right. Of course he was right.

Another tear joined the second, falling to stain the silk of her gown. 'I don't care if you don't love me back.' She had to say it so he knew. 'I don't care about me. I only want what's best for you.'

Just for a second the cold diamond of his eyes flared as his gaze tracked her tears. 'But you should care,' he said suddenly, low and fierce. 'And you should have someone who can give you what's best for you too.'

She brushed away a tear, not caring where it fell, not understanding. 'What do you mean?'

Tiberius muttered a low curse, that muscle in his jaw leaping. 'I mean that I should never have married you, Guinevere Accorsi. You'd have been better off if I'd just let you go.'

Guinevere stared up at him in shock, her heart feeling as if it was full of broken glass. 'But I wouldn't,' she whispered. 'I would have been still hiding in the walls, too afraid to come out.'

He said nothing to that, only stared at her for one long, aching moment.

Then he turned on his heel and left her standing alone by the column.

CHAPTER TWELVE

TIBERIUS PUSHED HIS WAY through the crowd, abruptly unable to bear being in the ballroom any longer. A hot, painful feeling was pressing against his chest, making it feel as if he was suffocating, and he was desperate to get outside and breathe the cold mountain air.

He found some doors that led to an outside terrace and managed to get them open, stepping out into the clear night, his chest heaving.

But even taking deep breaths of the cold Swiss night didn't relieve the burning sensation, or the tightness. It was as if something enormous was sitting on his sternum.

It was all to do with Guinevere, and he knew it.

Her dark blue eyes looking up at him as she told him that she was in love with him. The wild rush of joy that had filled his veins in that moment, and then the aching bitterness that had followed it, because love wasn't for kings. Or at least not the kind of love that she deserved.

He'd hurt her, bastard that he was. He'd made her cry. He'd told her that she would be better off without him, and she would. She needed someone who could give her their whole heart, not just a small piece of it.

She'd had nothing all her life—nothing but her brothers' fists and her father's indifference. It was incredible how her bright, warm, effervescent spirit hadn't buckled under the fear and violence she'd experienced, or at least crumbled away.

But it hadn't.

Despite how her father and brothers had treated her, she was undaunted. And he'd watched her turn from a mouse into a lioness, all beautiful, strong, brave and caring.

A woman like that deserved the entire world—not to be tied to a man who'd never be able to put her first. A man who'd never tasted happiness and had no idea what joy looked like. What could he offer her? Pleasure in bed, that was all.

He walked over to the stone parapet and gripped it, looking out over the lake at the mountains looming dark and forbidding in the night, the caps of snow gleaming.

He didn't know where that left him.

Divorcing her felt impossible, and yet that was the only option he could see. The only option that would give her the freedom she needed and deserved. Freedom from him and from Kasimir.

Free to make her own choices—choices that hadn't been forced on her the way he'd forced them on her at the very beginning, by demanding that she marry him, that she pay for her family's crimes.

The pain in his chest deepened, excoriating him.

He couldn't bear the thought of letting her go, and yet he had to.

To be a ruler required sacrifice, his father had told

him. Both of his parents had made that sacrifice. And so would he.

He had to follow their example, otherwise what was he?

An empty, hollow man. A man without purpose, whose whole life had been for nothing.

Tiberius stepped back from the parapet. He'd go and find her now and tell her that she had to leave him, that she should be free, and he had to do it quickly. Make it swift and hard, like ripping off a sticking plaster, so she could heal faster.

He turned around, moved back to the doors.

And found Guinevere standing there, shining in the moonlight, sparkling and glittering like the fairy she was, her eyes, dark in the night, burning with her lioness courage.

He froze, the pain in his chest an agony. 'I told you we'd have this conversation later,' he said, his voice rough and raw.

'It is later,' she said levelly, and stepped outside into the night. 'But we don't need to have this conversation at all. You've said your piece, I've said mine, and we'll agree to disagree.'

That was not what he'd expected.

'Guinevere,' he said, forcing the word out. 'I have made a decision. I can't give you what you need, and as such I can't ask you to stay with me. So I'm going to start divorce proceedings—'

'No,' she interrupted flatly, and crossed the space between them, coming straight up to him and putting her arms around him, her head on his chest. 'You can start proceedings, if you want, but I'm not leaving you. I'm never leaving you.'

He couldn't bear to push her away, yet he also couldn't bear to touch her because if he did, he knew he'd never let her go.

'You have to.' His voice was wooden. 'You deserve a man who can love you the way—'

'And I have found him,' she interrupted yet again, lifting her head and looking up at him. 'What I deserve is to be with the man I love, and that's you. So, no. I'm not leaving, Tiberius.'

His heart felt like it was chained in barbed wire, little hooks digging into it, tearing it. 'Lioness, I can't...'

'I'm not going to ask you to put me first,' she said. 'I would never ask that of you. All I want is a little corner of your heart that is mine. That's all.'

A little corner of his heart...

'Guinevere...'

'You love an entire country,' she said. 'Are you telling me you really can't spare a small piece of that great heart of yours?'

He looked down into her eyes and he could feel the fear wrapping around him, squeezing tight. The fear that she hadn't just claimed a small piece, that she'd claimed all of it. All of him. And he was afraid, because where did that leave him?

'If I love you,' he began roughly, 'then what is there left for Kasimir?'

Her eyes were midnight-blue and her arms around him were warm as she said, 'Why do you think love is limited? That if you give it to your country there's nothing left for anything else? Think bigger, my king. Love is boundless. I can love you and love my country. It's just a different kind of love.'

His will was fading, his strength to put her from him failing. 'I can't make you happy, Guinevere. I don't even know what that looks like.'

Strangely, she smiled at him. 'Yes, you do. It's me and you in the orchard, lying on our backs and looking at the stars.'

She's right.

It burst through him then, in a brilliant flash of light. Yes, he *had* been happy with her that day in the orchard. He'd been happy with her in every one of their daily two-hour meetings, and he'd been happy because of her. Because she'd showed him what it felt like. And it was lying on his back with her in his arms, looking at the stars. It was her in his lap, kissing him and touching him as if he was precious.

It was her smile—the one she gave him every day— and it was her in her yellow dress, looking like a splash of sunshine.

And it was her, her eyes dark, telling him she loved him.

She was happiness.

Which must mean that the agonising pressure in his heart was love.

Because he did love her, even though he'd been telling himself he didn't. Even though he'd been telling himself it was impossible to love her and his country at the same time.

In fact it was perfectly possible, and he'd been doing it for at least a couple of weeks now.

He lifted his hands and cupped her face between them. 'Guinevere…little lioness…it cannot be just about me. You need happiness in your life too. You *deserve* it.'

Guinevere looked up into his beautiful face, her arms tight around his narrow waist. There was anguish there, and something fierce and hot and bright.

Her king. Her enemy. Her husband.

The man she loved without limit and without reservation.

She'd known that the minute he'd walked away from her, leaving her standing alone in the ballroom. After telling her that he couldn't give her what she deserved and that she'd be better off if she'd never met him.

But she'd told him the truth—that she'd still have been hiding in the walls if he hadn't come along and shown her the courage that had always been there inside her.

And as he'd walked away from her she'd known she couldn't let him. That he needed to learn a lesson too, and one that only she could teach him.

A lesson about the love she knew lay in his heart. The love for his parents that had translated into a driving need to make their deaths matter. The love for his country and for his people that had kept him on the path to the crown.

This king was made of love. And it wasn't a distraction. And loving his country didn't mean he couldn't love her.

Not that she needed him to love her, she'd decided as his tall form disappeared in the crowded ballroom. It didn't matter in the end. Because what she wanted was his happiness, and that was all that mattered to her. He had no one. His parents were gone, he had no siblings, no friends. He was an island, in splendid isolation, and she was his only bridge.

He might decide to divorce her and he probably would—'for her own good'. But she didn't care if he did. She wasn't going to leave him. She couldn't leave him. And she'd rather be trapped inside the walls of the palace with him than be free to go wherever she wanted, because his happiness was her happiness and there was no freedom without him.

So she'd gone after him, to tell him that she wouldn't be leaving him, and had found him on the balcony alone, a look of despair on his face.

He'd muttered something about divorce, but she'd ignored that, showing him, then telling him, that she wasn't going to leave.

Her heart felt barbed and sharp, but the pain wasn't as bad as when she'd stood in the ballroom, because she'd made a decision. It hurt now, though, with his warm palms against her cheek, his expression fierce, silver eyes blazing as he told her she deserved happiness.

'Yes,' she said. 'I do. And luckily I already have it here with you.'

'Guinevere…'

'You make me happy, my king. And you don't need to do anything more and you don't need to be anything else. Just you, as you are.'

'Two hours a day,' he said roughly. 'You wanted more than two hours.'

She tightened her arms around him, holding him fast. 'If you can only give me two hours, then I will be happy with that.' Her eyes prickled with the force of her emotions. 'I will never be happy without you, Tiberius. Don't you understand that?'

The look on his face intensified, and the silver flames in his eyes burned impossibly bright, and for a long time he just looked down at her. Then he said, his voice hot and deep, 'You told me that love isn't something that's finite and I think you're right. I've been afraid that I can't love you and my country at the same time, but I think I've been doing so for the past two weeks.'

A hot wash of shock went through her, her painful heart igniting into flame. 'You...love me?'

Tiberius smiled, natural and brilliant, like the sun coming out. 'Yes, little lioness. I love you.' Then he bent his head and kissed her, his mouth hot and demanding, and when he came up for air, he growled, 'Two hours, my queen. I demand two hours of your time every day. Two hours for the rest of my life.'

'Two hours? My king, I will give you eternity.'

And she did.

EPILOGUE

'THERE,' TIBERIUS SAID, adjusting the telescope. 'Can you see Venus? It's very bright.'

Standing beside him under the orange trees, on the grass of the orchard, his lioness peered through the high-powered telescope Tiberius had brought with him.

'Oh, yes!' she exclaimed in wonder. 'You're right. It's amazingly bright.'

It was their little ritual—to come out here at night once a month, to look at the stars and remind themselves of the whole beautiful universe that they were only tiny parts of.

Plus, Tiberius simply liked astronomy, and had been pursuing it whenever he had a moment. Which was more often than he'd expected.

Being a king was hard work, as his father had said, but it was work that he shared with his lovely wife—and a burden shared was a burden halved.

He glanced down at the baby who slept peacefully in the crook of his arm. His gorgeous daughter and his heir, barely three weeks old and already proving to be a lioness, just like her mother.

He'd thought it wasn't possible to love his wife and

his country at the same time, but it was eminently possible. Just as it was possible for that love to grow to include his new daughter, and any more children they would have together.

And there would be more. He'd already decided.

Love expands, he thought, slipping his free arm around his wife, and holding her close.

Love was as infinite as the stars.

* * * * *

Were you blown away by
King, Enemy, Husband?
Then why not explore these other steamy reads
from Jackie Ashenden?

Spanish Marriage Solution
Italian Baby Shock
The Twins That Bind
Boss's Heir Demand
Newlywed Enemies

Available now!

HARLEQUIN
Reader Service

Enjoyed your book?

Try the perfect subscription for Romance readers and get more great books like this delivered right to your door.

See why over 10+ million readers have tried Harlequin Reader Service.

Start with a Free Welcome Collection with free books and a gift—valued over $20.

Choose any series in print or ebook. See website for details and order today:

TryReaderService.com/subscriptions